ANNE HAMPSON

Stardust

Silhouette Romance

Published by Silhouette Books

Copyright © 1982 by Filestone Limited
and Silhouette Books, a Simon & Schuster
division of Gulf & Western Corporation

Map by Tony Ferrara

First printing 1982

British Library C.I.P.

Hampson, Anne
   Stardust.—(Silhouette romance)
   I. Title
   823'.914[F]   PR6058.A5547

ISBN 0 340 32692 1

Printed and bound in Great Britain for
Hodder and Stoughton Paperbacks, a
division of Hodder and Stoughton Ltd.,
Mill Road, Dunton Green, Sevenoaks,
Kent (Editorial Office: 47 Bedford
Square, London, WC1 3DP) by
Richard Clay (The Chaucer Press) Ltd.,
Bungay, Suffolk

Stardust

Chapter One

It was with an inescapable premonition of doom uppermost in her mind that Jody entered the sanctum of what had, until recently, been her adoptive father's study. Rochelle, 'golden-girl' winner of two beauty competitions and idol of all the male members of the various clubs to which she belonged, was sitting at the ancient leather-topped desk, perusing an open ledger, so totally absorbed in it that she seemed not to be aware of her sister's presence. Or perhaps, thought Jody, she was being deliberately ungracious, which would be the rule rather than the exception.

'Mary said you wanted to see me.' Jody moved slowly forward after closing the door, but she did not venture to sit down. It was inexplicable, this feeling of being a stranger in the house where she had lived for almost twelve years. 'Is it something important?'

A superfluous question born of nervousness which itself resulted from the nameless fear and uncertainty which had burst upon her a few moments ago when Mary had come to her in the garden and said, unsteadily and with a frown on her brow, 'Rochelle wants you in the study. She was even more uncivil than usual, and I think you'd better not keep her waiting.'

Mary had paused as if on the point of adding something more, but with a shake of her head she had walked away, briskly proceeding to the side door leading to the kitchen.

'Mary seemed a little agitated—'

'I've given her a month's notice,' broke in Rochelle impatiently.

'You . . . !' Jody shook her head in disbelief. 'I don't understand, Rochelle—'

'You will in a moment.' Rochelle's lovely blue eyes flickered over Jody's immature figure in a cursory examination, while Jody's own eyes remained on her sister's face; she was wondering why no one had ever managed to catch the icy glitter which sometimes marred the real beauty of those eyes, or questioned the sincerity of Rochelle's disarming smile. Certainly Philip and Monica Hendrick had had no suspicions, hence their leaving the valuable Victorian house and its contents to the elder of their adopted children. As memory touched the edge of Jody's mind, she found herself reliving numerous incidents in which she had known a sense of exclusion, of being shut out, but always she had accepted this treatment as natural, her being so much younger than Rochelle, who always seemed able to hold her own in any conversation or discussion with her parents. For Jody there had never been this kind of comradeship, nor was there even a hazy recollection of a show of real love, and during the past few months she had often sensed a regret about her parents as to the wisdom of their adopting a second child when they already had one who, at eleven years old, had been with them almost from birth. Although only six at the time, Jody had recognised the fierce jealousy which at first characterised Rochelle's attitude towards her. It was as if, instead of welcoming a sister, Rochelle had regarded Jody as a potential competitor for the affections of their adoptive parents. Portraying a cleverness beyond her years, Rochelle had managed successfully to hide her animosity from them, being an affectionate and protective elder sister when in their company. Yet despite these disturbing attitudes of all three, Jody had never felt any sense of insecurity . . . not until now.

'I've decided to sell this house.' Rochelle's low, husky voice was hard—not at all the voice she used when speaking to one of her numerous admirers. 'I'm buying a small flat—a one-bedroom flat,' she added significantly, a thin smile curving her mouth as she noticed the colour leave her sister's face. 'It'll be about eight weeks before everything's settled, so you have plenty of time to get yourself fixed up. I've had an assurance from the estate agent that the house will sell quickly; it's the kind that's easily converted into flats, and you know how great a demand there is for them in this area.'

Stunned in spite of her previous misgivings, Jody could only stare wordlessly for a long moment before saying in a choked little voice, 'I can't understand why our parents left almost everything to you and nothing to me. It wasn't fair—'

'They didn't leave you anything simply because you've never helped them in their business. It was I who assisted Father, taking over the bookkeeping, looking after the office side of it generally.'

This was true, of course. In addition to her exquisite beauty, Rochelle had been gifted with a brilliant mind which her father used in his decorating firm from the time Rochelle left school at sixteen years of age. She practically ran the business, and it was because Philip could trust her to look after things that he and his wife decided to take a holiday in the Far East. A small airplane carrying them from Singapore to a tiny island where they intended staying for a few days crashed with the loss of all passengers and crew. That was six weeks ago, and ever since the will was read, Jody had observed a change in her sister, the growing arrogance, the attitude of complete superiority she had assumed.

And now the bombshell had come. Jody was being turned out of the house. Again incidents and sensations spread out from the mists of memory—the feeling of not belonging, the lack of love, the awareness of being a flaw in the pattern of life in the lovely home which now belonged entirely to her adoptive sister, the girl who was speaking again, repeating what she had said in order to emphasize it. Jody looked at her through a mist of tears.

'I know you ran the office all on your own, Rochelle, but you're five years older than I. They let you leave school at sixteen and enter the business.'

'Could you have left at sixteen and entered the business?' was Rochelle's disparaging response to that. 'You haven't the brain.'

'I hoped to get my A-levels!' flashed Jody indignantly.

'Hoped?' with a lift of Rochelle's delicate eyebrows. 'You'd not have succeeded, and I did tell Father it was a waste of time and money, keeping you at school. He ought to have sent you into a shop or something. The experience would have served you in good stead at this present time.'

'They never did like me as much as you!' The protest was vehement but yet tearful, for although Jody bitterly resented what her parents had done, she had by no means recovered from the shock of their sudden death. For her a void had been left which she felt would be a long while in closing, whereas Rochelle had never even shed a tear or spoken one word of regret.

'That assertion,' returned Rochelle hardly, 'is pure imagination on your part.'

'Then why didn't they treat us both alike when they made their will?'

'As they're not here to explain, your question's absurd.' A frown darkened Rochelle's wide brow as she waited for Jody to comment. But Jody was dumb, her mind trying to grapple with this situation in which, at only eighteen, she was being turned out of her home—with practically nothing, for the small legacy left to her could not possibly provide her with even the smallest apartment. She could rent one, she supposed, and the money would buy the furniture, but what then? Jody was still at school, about to take her A-levels, after which she would have gone on to secretarial school. These were the plans her parents had made for her and which she had accepted, ever filled with gratitude, first for their adopting her, and second for everything they had done for her since.

'I don't expect they thought they'd die for a long time yet,' murmured Jody at last, speaking her thoughts aloud.

'No,' agreed Rochelle unemotionally, 'I don't expect they did.'

Again Jody looked directly at her, and suddenly

she was enveloped in a great sadness, a sadness transcending the fear, the knowledge of being alone in the world and the dazed floundering of a mind desperately groping for some kind of picture of the future, some form of light to which she could reach out.

Yes, it was sadness which held her as, wordlessly, she left the study and made her way through the house, nodding to Mary in sympathy but too weighed down to express the concern she ought to have voiced. She was dwelling on all she had missed —the love of parents and a sister. If only she had been given that love, everything would have been so different. She and Rochelle would have shared the house and the money which Rochelle was receiving from the sale of the business, and they would have continued to live together, comforting one another, becoming even closer because of their loss.

Jody's thoughts changed, and she was thinking of Mary, who had been with the Hendricks for over twenty years, and who, like Jody, had no one else in the world. But she was well past middle age and she had been thrifty. She had once told Jody of her ambition to have a cottage in the country where she could grow flowers and vegetables and keep fowl.

Just like Old Bill, mused Jody as she covered the wide, immaculate lawn slowly, making for the little prefabricated house in the trees where the garden bordered the one next door.

The gentle shadows of a May evening were spreading over the wooded part of the gardens as the tiny prefab came into her line of vision, its drab grey walls damp-stained, its window frames slightly askew. Old Bill was sitting on a rough bench outside the open door, and Jody stopped a moment to stare and sigh, herself unseen, as with one hand he held a folded newspaper at some distance from his face, while the other arm dangled at his side. She glanced down at his feet, where his bare toes filled the holes in a pair of Philip's cast-off canvas shoes, and then she lifted her eyes again to take in the sparse hair, half grey, half pale sandy, lying in separated strands, wash-hungry and long. Seventy-six in two months' time. . . . He ought to be retiring anyway, thought Jody, but what would he do and where would he live? Yes, it needed no special sense of perception to realise that he, too, had been told to go. Affection surged in a great wave within her, and Jody quickened her steps. He glanced over the paper and she saw with a little access of tenderness that his spectacles—one of which was cracked within its metal frame—were, as usual, balanced lopsidedly on the very end of his nose. A smile broke through the forlorn set of his face as she drew closer.

'Hello, Bill.' Jody eased herself down on a boulder which, aeons of time ago, had been dropped by the ice and which no one had ever decided to move. 'How many eggs today?'

'Eight.' A pause, and then, 'You're not too bright, little Jody. Want to talk to Old Bill about it?'

Jody's big brown eyes were intent. 'You're not too bright either. Something's wrong?'

He paused, then shrugged his shoulders. 'Rochelle's selling up. I have to go.'

Tears spiked Jody's eyes, and her young mouth quivered uncontrollably. 'I knew it, of course. . . .' She swallowed the painful lump that had risen in her throat. 'It was inevitable, seeing that Rochelle's leaving. I don't suppose the new owners will want you any more than they'll want Mary.'

'And you, little one?' The tone held concern, deep concern, for Old Bill and Jody had always been close, confiding in one another, giving and being given sympathy that often amounted to deep affection. Both were starved of love, and for Jody the tiny home of two rooms and kitchen had been the haven to which she would run when things became too hurtful to bear. It was to Old Bill that she had come on hearing of the death of her adoptive parents, and on his shoulder she had wept.

'They were good to me in their own way,' she had said, clinging to Bill's coat despite the fact of its not being any too clean. 'Oh, why did it have to happen!'

Bill's soothing voice and touch, his gentleness—even the clumsy way he had kissed her—were balm to Jody's heart so that she scarcely noticed the total lack of affection and understanding on her sister's part.

'I have to go too,' answered Jody, returning her thoughts to his question. 'I don't know what to do.'

'I've never said much about Rochelle, but right from the first we didn't get along. She never could forget that I'd been a sort of vagabond, wandering about without a roof over my head. It was Mr. Hendrick who took me in one day after I'd knocked on his door and asked if he wanted his lawn cut. He'd had a man who let him down several times, so he said yes, I could cut the lawn, and he gave me a few shillings, as our money was at that time.' Old Bill paused reflectively. 'I said I'd come the following week, which I did, and then he offered me a permanent job doing the garden, and after I'd got settled in the little prefab he'd bought, I began to keep the hens and ducks.'

He paused again, and Jody glanced around, her troubles forgotten momentarily as her eyes wandered from the neat rows of peas and beans to the healthy foliage of the potatoes. And away in a

secluded corner was the hencote, with the birds
scratching about for worms and grit. The ducks were
on a small pond at the far end of the long garden;
Jody could hear them quacking and vaguely wondered how many eggs were lost by being laid in the
water. Or perhaps ducks did not lay in the water.
Jody did not know.

'I shall have to leave school,' she murmured, her
thoughts brought starkly back to the present by the
glimpse she had of Mary pegging out the tea towels
on the little line at the back of the house. 'I was so
optimistic about getting my A-levels.' Jody's eyes
were heavily shadowed; looking at her, Old Bill
knew of the fear that was threading its way through
her mind.

'I wish I had some money.' It was the first time
Jody had ever heard Old Bill say anything like that.
She knew how much he received for his work. It was
a mere pittance, but he was content because he had
his garden and the fowl. He provided the household
with vegetables and poultry but had more than
enough left over for himself, and he lived well. 'I'd
give it to you so that you could buy a little
home. . . .' His voice trailed off as a frown creased
his forehead. A gnarled hand stroked the jutting
chin, and he was shaking his head. 'We're in a mess,
little Jody,' he ended, and she closed her eyes tightly
to hold back a deluge of tears.

'I can't think straight,' she said.

'It's not so bad for me.' Old Bill's face grew
thoughtful. 'I can go back to the road—'

'Oh, no!' cried Jody, distressed and tearful. 'Not
at your age, Bill!'

'What else is there for me?' he demanded, and his
tone was calm and philosophical. 'I've had it good
for a number of years, so where's my grumble?'

The tears escaped and ran down Jody's cheeks. 'You can be helped by the state; you know that.'

'Charity?' Bill shook his head. 'Not for me. I shall take to the road again and keep my pride.' He looked at her from above the steel rims of his spectacles, inviting further comment, but Jody said nothing. 'That Rochelle,' he added after a while, 'could not even tell me politely to leave. She treated me as if I were nothing more than a worm wriggling about her feet.' Again Jody said nothing, because she knew he was right. Rochelle had always looked down on Old Bill, calling him a tramp and ne'er-do-well. But Jody knew of his misfortunes, knew how, having been born to dire poverty, he was orphaned at the age of twelve and taken by an uncle who made him work in his coal-delivery business, forcing him to heave the heavy bags even though he was a mere child still. After two years he ran away and for a while worked on ships, but then he was ill, and moved about the countryside, almost dying on his feet. A farmer found him in his barn early one morning, and from then on Bill was taken care of by the farmer's wife, who provided him with a bed in the attic. He was happy working on the farm, but eventually the farmer grew too old to keep it on and the people to whom he sold it did not want anyone living in, and although Bill said he was willing to sleep in the barn, they would not allow it. And so Bill took to the road, enjoying the freedom even while appreciating the fact that life could not continue like that. So when he was offered the job by Philip Hendrick, he accepted eagerly, happy to have a roof of his own at last. It was sparsely furnished, with only the bare necessities, but every Christmas he had received presents from Monica and Philip, and from Jody, useful things, often for his kitchen;

Jody's present last Christmas was a bright blue tablecloth, and her mother had given him some cutlery and a cruet.

And now Old Bill had to leave it all . . . and take to the road again. At seventy-six. . . .

'If only our parents had split everything between us, Bill, then I would have insisted that you stay.'

'I was staggered when I knew of that will. But always you were eclipsed by Rochelle, so I ought to have expected something of the sort happening over the property.' Old Bill's voice was gruff, and edged with concern for Jody's plight.

'I expect they assumed I'd be married before they died.'

'In the ordinary way, you would have been, but they ought to have treated you both alike in any case.'

'What are we to do, Bill?' Several ideas now careered into Jody's mind: she could go into what was at one time called 'service'—and live in and be someone's servant. Or she could perhaps do some kind of hotel work where accommodation would count as part of her salary. To live among strangers, though, and to be at their beck and call, for that was how it was when you lived in . . . there was no getting away from your work.

She cast a glance at Old Bill, thinking he had dozed off, but he was staring into space, his eyes pale lavender above his lopsided spectacles. Rising slowly, she left him to his silence and made her way back to the house.

Rochelle was going away for a week's holiday. It was a snap decision made when she was asked by a friend to take the place of the girl who had let her down.

'I'll expect you to have made some arrangements when I get back,' Rochelle warned Jody. 'The house is sold and the people are only waiting for the mortgage to come through.'

'But, Rochelle, where can I go?'

"It's not my affair.'

'You're my sister—'

'Don't be absurd. We're totally unrelated.'

'So you don't care what happens to . . . to me?' Jody knew she was lacking in courage, knew that someone stronger and more self-reliant would tackle this problem as it should be tackled—bravely and with the determination to win through. But try as she would, Jody could not rid herself of this feeling of helplessness, and as she had said to Old Bill, she could not think straight. She continued to flounder, even though it was possible that the new owners would be taking possession in three or four weeks' time.

'Why should I care what happens to you?' Rochelle was frowning, and for a hopeful moment Jody had the impression that she was troubled about her. However, Rochelle's next words soon disillusioned her on that particular score. 'I've my own life to make, Jody. I'm out of a job now, remember, and it might take me some time to find one. Meanwhile, I have to settle myself in the flat I've bought—it needs decorating and furnishing. So you can see that I have enough on my mind without taking on the responsibility of a child who is not even related to me.'

Jody remained dumb, since there was nothing to say—nothing that would do her any good, that is, so why waste words?

Yet on the day when Rochelle was in her room packing the two smart suitcases she had bought herself, Jody knocked gently and entered, then spoke swiftly as if by so doing she could touch a soft spot somewhere in her adoptive sister's makeup.

'Rochelle, if you would let me live with you in your flat, just until I've taken my exams and left school, I might be able to find a job and—'

'I've already told you, the flat has only one bedroom.' Curt the tone, and accompanied by a sweeping glance that was both contemptuous and impatient. 'You're eighteen,' went on Rochelle as she folded a gay cotton dress and put it carefully on top of several others. 'Many girls of your age fend for themselves.'

'Yes, I know,' agreed Jody, but went on to say that she had not yet left school, much less been trained for any job. 'Who's going to employ me when I've no experience at anything?'

'That,' answered Rochelle with some asperity, 'is your affair entirely. And now, will you go, and let me get on with this packing? I have to be at the airport in less than three hours' time.'

Half an hour later Old Bill was asking where Rochelle was going for her holiday.

'Portugal. I'd love to go abroad.' A wistful expression erased the stress from Jody's face, and the old man caught his breath. Long ago he had predicted that Jody would be even more beautiful then her sister, and now that beauty was fast developing. Those eyes, so soft and brown, were enhanced by thick curling lashes which seemed to the old man to have grown overnight; the silken hair had grown too; it was slightly waved and flicked up in half-curls resting on her delicately sloping shoulders. Her features had a classical quality about them that reminded him of a Greek *kore*, and her skin was like flawless alabaster, translucent over the blue veins at her temples. She parted her rosy lips and smiled, and he nodded over and over again. Yes, her beauty was about to open, like that of a rose unfurling its tender petals to the sun. And her beauty would last, because it was deep. Rochelle's would fade, destroyed by the ice beneath its delicate surface.

'Bill, what are you thinking about?' Jody moved over to a chair and sat down.

'You,' answered Old Bill briefly.

'Yes, of course. You're wondering what is to become of me.'

He said nothing to that, and for a long while they sat in silence, each trying to envisage the future.

'Something might turn up,' said Old Bill at last, and Jody gave a sigh, for it was an impossibility for anything to turn up.

But little did she know with what stunning effect those words were to come back to her, and before very long.

Rochelle had been away only two days when the letter arrived.

'From a solicitor,' murmured Jody with a frown and an almost fearful hesitancy about opening it.

Ten minutes later she was at the telephone, obeying the request made to her in the letter, and a quarter of an hour after that she was racing across the smooth lawn, hair flying.

'Bill,' she gasped, waving the letter in the breeze. 'Bill, we're saved! I've inherited half a castle in Ireland—I did tell you I was part Irish, didn't I? It was on my mother's side. Bill, are you listening to me?'

'Well, now, yes and no, young Jody. People don't inherit half a castle; it has to be a whole one or nothing at all. Sit down and get your breath back.'

'Another person already owns the other half—he was a partner in this hotel—'

'Hotel?'

'The castle was turned into an hotel years ago and I own half of it! I have to see the solicitor at ten o'clock in the morning. Oh, Bill, you did predict that something would happen, remember?'

'I did, but it was only for something to say.'

'Well, it's come true! And you're coming with me to Ireland. There'll be lots of things you'll like to do at a castle!"

'Maybe I'd not be wanted by this other person.'

Jody's head lifted. She was very sure that she was part-owner of this castle, because the solicitor had convinced her of it. And she was also very sure that Bill was going to Ireland with her, no matter whether this other person wanted him or not.

Chapter Two

The car slowed down, then stopped at the gate. On
an imposing blue-and-gold plaque fixed to one of the
gateposts Jody read 'Rushwood Castle Hotel,' and a
long deep sigh seemed to escape from the very heart
of her.

'Is it true?' she whispered to the old man sitting
beside her in the back of the cab which had brought
them from Shannon Airport. Old Bill was either too
awed or too uncomfortable to reply, and in any case,
a uniformed attendant emerged from the interior of
an ivy-clad stone lodge to ask if they were staying in
the hotel.

'I'm Miss Jody Hendrick, and I'm expected.' Jody
leant towards the open window to scan the man's
weather-worn face. He was smiling suddenly, examining her with interest.

'Of course, Miss Hendrick.' The gate swung open

for the car to enter the long, curving tree-lined driveway to the castle.

'Have you ever seen anything like it, Bill?' Fleetingly a sense of unease cast a shadow over Jody's previous excitement, and her stomach muscles were twisting themselves into hard little knots. There was still no answer from the man in the corner. He just sat there looking inexpressibly uncomfortable in the smart grey suit he was wearing, and several times Jody had seen him running a bony finger inside the collar of his immaculate white shirt. For the whole hour and a half in the airplane he had sat erect, just as if he were confined within a straitjacket and could not move.

'I daresay I shan't like it,' he sighed at last as the car bowled along the avenue of trees to skirt a picturesque golf course where several of the hotel guests were playing, their holiday clothes bright and colourful in the sunshine. Massive trees abounded all over the beautiful grounds, and as the car drew closer to the magnificent castellated mansion, the gleaming island-studded waters of Lough Corrib came into view, set against the dramatic backdrop of the mountains of Connemara to the west. Jody gasped audibly, and even Old Bill stirred himself to show interest.

'I can't believe it's really happening,' breathed Jody, clutching her handbag as if in the gesture she would find support. 'How has it all happened, Bill, and to me?' It was natural that she should think of the house in which she lived and which now belonged to Rochelle, and it was natural that she should compare the two. And of course, there was no comparison.

The car swung over a cut-stone bridge across the

shining river, then passed through a high, turreted gateway before coming to a smooth halt outside the impressive front entrance to the hotel.

'Perhaps I shall like it after all,' conceded Bill, but there was little enthusiasm in his voice, and he did decide to add, 'But I don't know why I let you persuade me to come on this visit, little Jody, seeing it's only for a day or so.'

'I couldn't come alone,' she said reasonably. 'Besides, Mr. Thorpe, the solicitor, said I ought to have someone with me.'

'You could have waited till Rochelle was home, and she could have come. She has the sort of business head I think you'll need when dealing with this Irish fellow. They're a wild lot, and they keep their women under—that's a known fact, even in these days of women's liberation, and I'm worried, lass, that you'll be browbeaten by this man who owns the other half of this hotel. He'll not like the idea of a female partner, especially a child like you!'

Jody was worried too, but she had no intention of admitting it, either to Old Bill or to anyone else. But if she had it to do over again, she most certainly would have waited those few extra days so that she could have asked Rochelle to come over here with her. It had been an impulsive decision made simply because she had her back to the wall, her frightened mind a surging mass of chaotic thoughts and ideas as to what she must do about her future. Out of the blue the letter had arrived, and she found she was the owner of half a castle. It was nothing less than a miracle, and Jody had acted impetuously, half-fearing that if she delayed, the whole thing would turn out to be a dream. And in this state of urgency it never crossed her mind to wait for Rochelle's return.

Poor Bill, she mused as she slid from the taxi onto the gravel. He had certainly taken some persuading, because, like Jody herself, he had never flown in an airplane. But she had been strong in her insistence, assuring him of a home and security for the rest of his life, and at last he had succumbed. But to get him into the suit was something else, and even now, when she was filled with trepidation about the forthcoming meeting with her partner, Jody had to smile at the recollection of Old Bill's face when she presented him with the new clothes, which she had bought out of the legacy.

She turned to look at him as he walked from the car towards the massive oak door of the main entrance which led into the lobby of the hotel. There was a sombre air about him, a woebegone expression in his pale watery eyes. And he was limping in the shining new shoes he wore.

'Do you think I could change?' he asked, one eye watching the driver as he took out the two brand-new suitcases, the smaller of which was Old Bill's. 'I'd be more myself in my own clothes.'

'You can't change yet,' broke in Jody, wishing now that she hadn't let him bring all those old clothes with him. But, like her, he had been insistent—and to the point of blackmail; it had become a case of 'let me bring my clothes or I don't come.'

Jody paid the taxi driver, then stood for a space taking stock of her surroundings, a sort of awed wonderment pervading her senses when eventually she lifted her eyes to scan the magnificent spectacle of the castle itself. It was beautiful, but she realised at once that only part of it was really ancient. Several additions had been made, but with both delicacy and finesse, so that the whole blended harmoniously, perfect in structure and style. A great thrill of pleasure rose to erase all her misgivings. It still seemed impossible that she owned half of so valuable an establishment, but Mr. Thorpe had convinced her that it was so.

'The porter's taking our luggage in.' Old Bill's voice recalled her, and she turned to follow the uniformed man into the lobby. Although dazed by all the elegance and splendour, she managed to retain her composure, to hold on to a part of that serene detachment which had come to her when she had fully realised that her future was safe, that she had a home to go to, and security as well.

Nevertheless, it was inevitable that she should feel small and faintly unsure of herself as she stood under the towering, ornately stuccoed ceiling, waiting for the receptionist to come to her. Tall and smiling, he asked her name, and showed no real surprise when she told him.

'Mr. Blake is expecting you, Miss Hendrick. . . .' He paused as his eyes lit on Old Bill, standing there on one foot, the other pressed against the back of his leg, an expression of acute discomfort on his lined and pallid face. 'This is the gentleman who came with you?'

'Yes, Mr. Stephenson. My solicitor phoned to tell you I'd have my friend with me. Can he be shown to his room at once, please?'

'Of course, Miss Hendrick,' agreed the man respectfully. 'But first, I have instructions to show you into Mr. Blake's office the moment you arrive. My colleague will see to Mr. Stephenson.' Not a muscle moved in the man's face as he glanced at Old Bill, an almost ludicrous figure against the grace and elegance of what once had been the great hall of the castle.

'Thank you.' Jody smiled, and turning to Old Bill,

said, 'You'll be all right in a few minutes. But if you change your clothes, then don't leave your room, will you?'

'I wouldn't think of it—not in my ordinary clothes and shoes.'

There was a twinkle in his eyes now that made Jody say, 'You didn't bring those old shoes you were wearing the other day, surely?'

'They're very comfortable, with those holes in the toes—'

'If you will come this way, Miss Hendrick, I will take you to Mr. Blake.'

Jody swung around, said a swift word to Old Bill, then followed the receptionist through the lobby into a wide corridor towards a door at the far end. Her heart began to race as she waited a few seconds after the man had knocked on the heavy studded door.

'Come in.'

Jody knew a moment of panic as the man opened the door, but she managed to go forward quite steadily on legs that had become suddenly weak. The man announced her and withdrew.

Although she had naturally tried to form a picture of what her partner would look like, and decided he would be a cultured, aristocratic gentleman, Jody was totally unprepared for the superlative quality of looks and physique which met her eyes as, having risen from his chair and moved so that the massive oak desk would not be between them, Conor Blake stood there looking down at her from his impressive height. Feeling somewhat disorganised by his air of superiority and self-assurance, Jody swallowed nervously and waited for him to speak. But he seemed keenly interested in everything about her as his eyes, dark as a weathered meteorite, took in the delicate contours of her face, the clear high forehead above perfectly arched brows, the big brown eyes framed by thick curling lashes. Jody coloured beneath the cool, measured glance as Conor Blake's eyes roved, slowly and almost sensuously, over the curves of her body. She was not used to men, much less to their interest, and she felt stripped, with an almost irrepressible urge to run to the window and wrap one of the crimson velvet drapes about her body, hiding it from his probing search. Instead, she found herself making her own examination, aware of a long lean frame beneath perfectly cut grey slacks and a matching jacket cut on casual lines, of a deeply bronzed face with features finely chiselled and severe, the high cheekbones lending prominence to the hollows beneath them and to the hard, inflexible lines of the jaw and thrusting chin. She noticed strands of grey in his dark brown hair and wondered how old he was. Twenty-nine or thirty, she estimated, even though he looked older. Her eyes fell to his hand, resting on the back of a chair; muscular and sensitive like that of a pianist, she thought, aware of the startling contrast between its colour and the snow-white cuff of his shirt peeping from beneath the sleeve of the jacket. He spoke at last, apparently having seen all he wished to see.

'Miss Hendrick, I am Conor Blake.' He extended a hand to take hers; its crushing strength bound her slender fingers together for a few seconds after her hand was released. 'I trust you had a pleasant and uneventful flight from London?' The soft Irish brogue was far more pronounced than Jody had expected; it was a sudden delight to her sensitive ears, and somehow, her whole being was affected by it. The man was formidable, there was no doubt in her mind, but with a voice like that . . . Yes, her whole being was affected, and the little tug at her heart was beyond comprehension.

'Yes, thank you,' she answered shyly. 'It was a very smooth flight indeed, although we were delayed for an hour in London.'

'Sit down,' he invited, bypassing her comment. He indicated a chair, and she perched herself right on the edge, folding her hands together on her lap. 'Can I get you a drink of something?'

Jody shook her head. She felt constrained, touched by a sense of inadequacy. 'I'm not thirsty, thank you.'

'In that case,' he said, returning to his chair on the opposite side of the desk, 'we can begin to talk.' He sat down, and Jody was rather glad, because he tended to unnerve her, towering above her like that. She had never seen anyone quite so tall. Rochelle would like him, she mused idly, because Rochelle always went for tall men, being rather above average height herself. 'First, I must say that you are very young to have inherited so valuable a share in an hotel like this.'

'I'm eighteen,' she submitted, feeling inadequate and gauche.

'Eighteen?' with a lift of his eyebrows that might or might not have denoted mocking amusement, and Jody averted her face. How much more capable Rochelle would have been of handling this situation, she thought, again regretting her impulsiveness in coming here so quickly. 'Well, eighteen or no, you are my partner.' Conor seemed to sigh inwardly, and Jody could very well understand his feelings.

'I shan't be much good to you in helping to run this hotel, shall I?' she said, speaking her thoughts aloud.

'With the staff I have, the hotel runs very smoothly. There is no need for you to have anything to do
with the managing of it.' Abrupt the voice all at
once, and that attractive brogue seemed almost lost.
Jody looked at him across the desk; she saw the firm
set of his mouth, the dark gleam of determination
and authority in his eyes. It would never do to come
into collision with him, she thought, but had no
desire to do so anyway. 'I don't know how much
your solicitor told you,' he said, and looked interro-
gatingly at her, but for the present he gave her no
chance to reply as he continued, 'I've been in
constant touch with Mr. Thorpe since your great-
uncle's death. In fact, it was I who engaged him to
find the woman to whom Austin O'Rourke had left
his share of Rushwood Castle Hotel. Austin knew he
had a niece, but he had no idea she was dead, nor
that she had a child. However, you were soon found,
and as I've said, I have been in constant touch with
Mr. Thorpe.'

'So you know my background? I did tell him a
good deal, and I suppose he told you?'

Conor Blake nodded his head. 'We had a long
telephone conversation the day you called to see him
in answer to his letter.' Conor paused, and a slight
frown crossed his forehead. Jody thought of Old
Bill's prediction that he would not be happy with a
female partner and that he might browbeat her, but
as yet there had been no sign either that he resented
her or that he meant to intimidate her in any way.
She had the impression that he'd had an excellent
rapport with her great-uncle, Austin O'Rourke, and
in consequence he had to be gracious towards his
heir. 'Until I was told of your present plight, I had it
in mind to suggest that you stay in England and leave
the management to me, and I'd send you your share

every half-year. However, in view of your having to leave your home, it's best that you come to live here. You can take over Austin's private suite. It's at the end of the building and looks out onto the lough and its islands. You'll like it. It's one of the most luxurious and charming suites we have in the hotel. And now, you can answer my previous question. What did Mr. Thorpe tell you?'

'He told me that my mother's uncle and your father bought this castle years ago, when it was already an hotel.'

'That's correct.'

'Then your father died and you became my great-uncle's partner. Mr. Thorpe said that it was you who really managed the place during the last five years of my great-uncle's life, because he was in failing health.'

'That's right. But he was a grand old man. You'd have liked him, and it's a pity he didn't try to make contact many years ago. You'd probably have been with him instead of these people who adopted you. But it seems he didn't like your father . . .' Conor broke off and frowned. Whatever he knew, he was keeping to himself, and Jody silently thanked him for not saying anything against the father whom she remembered with affection even though she was only five years old when he died. Her mother died less than a year after him, and as she had never mentioned this uncle to anyone, it was believed that Jody had no relatives, hence her being taken into care and then adopted.

'I would have liked to know my great-uncle,' murmured Jody at last, a tinge of regret in her voice.

'He was a lonely old man . . .' Again he broke off, shrugging this time. 'What's done is done, and at least you are set up for life now.' For a moment he appeared to be more interested in the papers on his desk than in Jody, and she just sat quiet, watching him, noting again the handsome, finely etched features, the firm, dominant set of the jawline and mouth, the long-lashed eyes that lifted suddenly as if he was aware of her keen regard. She coloured delicately, but nothing in his expression gave evidence of his having noticed. 'I'm rather puzzled as to the reason why your adoptive parents left so much to your sister and only a small legacy to you.'

Embarrassed, Jody merely said, 'It was their decision and I had to abide by it.' No bitterness in her tone, but a certain sadness of which she was unaware but which was not missed by the man sitting opposite her. It arrested his attention so that his stare was searching and prolonged, and, disconcerted by it, Jody glanced away.

'Well, all your troubles are over now.' Conor spoke at last, in that soft Irish brogue, but in spite of its attractiveness, Jody thought she detected a hint of regret and wondered if he was disappointed that his original idea could not have materialised.

After a thoughtful moment she said, 'I'll not get in your way, Mr. Blake, and I hope you will just carry on as before—managing everything, that is. I don't want to interfere in any way.' The warm flush of embarrassment tinted her cheeks then, because she felt she had said the wrong thing. However, it passed without comment as he changed the subject, asking when she intended moving into the castle permanently.

'I believe you told Mr. Thorpe that the house you live in was already sold?'

'Yes, it is, and the new owners could be moving in within the next few weeks.'

'In that case, you'll want the suite quite soon. It

needs to be redecorated, so you can take a look at it and choose your colour scheme. How long will you be staying this time?'

'Only for one night, or perhaps two . . .' She looked uncertainly at him as if to discover whether or not it was convenient. He smiled faintly, in some amusement, and reminded her that as she was an equal partner, she had a right to stay as long as she liked. 'Then it'll be for two nights,' she said, a smile fluttering. 'But there's something I want to tell you about, Mr. Blake. It's Old Bill, the man who came with me. Er . . . he was a sort of tramp at one time . . .'

'Tramp?' with a swift frown of puzzlement.

Jody nodded her dark head. 'I would like him to come here to live. He's old but a very willing worker.' Jody's brown eyes were grave and anxious as they met his. 'He'll look after the poultry and the garden. . . .' Her glance strayed to the window, with its broad view over acres of manicured lawns and flower borders, wide shrubberies and neatly trimmed paths. 'Well, part of the garden,' she amended. 'Er . . . do you grow your own vegetables here?'

'We do, yes.'

'Then Old Bill will be eager to help. . . .' Again her voice trailed away to silence as she saw his expression. 'You don't like the idea?' A frown had settled on her forehead; she was wondering if she dared assert her rights as part owner of this property.

'How old is this . . . er . . . Old Bill?'

'Seventy-six, almost—but he's still able to work, Mr. Blake, so please let him come.' Swiftly she went on to relate the old man's story, and to her profound relief, she saw Conor's face soften slightly.

'Very well, he can come.'

'And you have a place for him to live—a little cottage or something?'

'There might be one vacant. I'll find out.' He seemed impatient now, and Jody rather thought it was because of Old Bill, and that Conor Blake didn't really want to have him. However, the concession had been made and she knew he would not go back on it. Jody hoped Old Bill would like his new job and settle in as easily as he had with her adoptive father. 'I'll have someone show you to your room.' Conor was already pressing a bell on his desk and glancing at his wristwatch at the same time. Jody suddenly felt flat, with that shut-out unwanted feeling she had known at home. Perhaps it was only that she was tired, she thought, turning her head as the door opened and a young girl entered in response to Conor's summons.

Chapter Three

Rochelle arrived back home at half-past three on the following Saturday afternoon, and was scarcely through the door when Jody said excitedly, 'I've some marvellous news to tell you, Rochelle! I've inherited a half-share in a castle in Ireland!'

'I'm not in the mood for fairy tales,' snapped Rochelle, picking up one of the suitcases which the taxi driver had dumped just inside the hall. 'The flight was awful—turbulence almost all the way. Make some tea; I'll be down in a few minutes when I've tidied myself up a bit.'

'I really have inherited half a castle,' Jody was saying twenty minutes later after she had poured the tea and handed Rochelle hers. 'Two days after you left, I had a letter. It's here; read it.' She passed it over, and staring at her with a frown of puzzlement and disbelief in her lovely eyes, Rochelle reached out to take it from her. 'I telephoned, then went to see this Mr. Thorpe,' Jody continued when Rochelle had read the letter and was handing it back. 'My mother's uncle owned half of this castle and he left it to her, so it came to me.' She continued, as briefly as she could, until Rochelle had the whole story. Jody did not know how Rochelle would take the news, and there was nothing in either her manner or her expression to reveal her thoughts, although she was keenly interested, especially when Jody talked about the owner of the other half, Conor Blake.

'And he's a bachelor, and really as handsome as you say?'

'He's exceptional, Rochelle! And the way he speaks—with a most attractive Irish brogue—and he's not at all arrogant, although you'd think he was to look at him, because he's so distinguished and . . . well, superior, sort of.'

'And he's to be your partner.' Soft the tone, inscrutable. Jody stared without knowing why, nor could she explain the quivering of a nerve in the pit of her stomach. Rochelle's face was a mask, but suddenly she produced a smile to which Jody responded, her stomach settling again.

'He already *is* my partner. Oh, Rochelle, you have no idea how happy I am! I had a beautiful bedroom—for two nights! And Mr. Blake was so nice to me! On both evenings we had dinner together in a huge dining room with beautiful furniture and Waterford chandeliers—and the food! You have never tasted anything like it! But of course, Rushwood Castle Hotel is internationally famous for its cuisine!' She paused, eyes shining . . . and she did not notice the cold gleam of envy in her listener's wide gaze. 'He showed me everything in the castle, and told me about the famous guests who come from all over the world, mainly America, because, after all, many Americans have Irish backgrounds. And guess what! I'm to have my great-uncle's private suite, where the sitting-room and bedroom windows have views of the lough!' Dreamily she recollected looking out from the window to the vast and hauntingly beautiful waters of the Corrib, with its numerous wooded islands floating like emeralds gleaming in a bed of soft velvet, and the highlands of Connemara, changing colours when the invading shadows of sunset turned the mauve to deep purple and the rose to russet brown. She remembered nighttime, too, when the moonlight lay cool and bright as silver on the tranquil, timeless waters of the lake. 'It must be the most beautiful scenery in the whole of Ireland,' added Jody enthusiastically.

'And you own half of this castle.' Rochelle's tone was low; she was talking to herself. 'It must be worth millions.'

Jody nodded at once. 'Several owners have added to it, each at great expense, and Mr. Blake was telling me that two of the rooms were built in honour of a visit to the castle by a king of England who stayed there for a whole month.'

'It must be famous, then.'

'I've just said so.' Pride edged Jody's voice, and a glint shone in Rochelle's eyes before they began to narrow slowly. She was lost in thought, and Jody seemed to sense an element of hostility in the silence. So it came as a complete surprise when Rochelle said, a warm smile on her lips, 'It sounds wonderful, Jody, and I do sincerely congratulate you. You're a most fortunate young woman, to become wealthy overnight.'

Jody looked at her for one uncertain moment, and then, strangely, she did not question her veracity. She must have been mistaken about that hostility, for nothing could be more open and genuine than the look in Rochelle's eyes as they met hers. Perhaps, thought Jody with a little access of happiness and hope, they might become good friends after all—real sisters, because, like her, Rochelle had no relatives. 'I'd love to see this castle,' went on Rochelle eagerly. 'When are you taking up residence?'

'In two weeks. Old Bill's there already. He went with me because I didn't want to go alone. And so he stayed.' A wry expression lit Jody's eyes as she added reflectively, 'He was quite overawed at first, and it was questionable as to whether he would stay. But when he was shown the lovely little stone cottage with its thatched roof which could be his, he made up his mind at once, and decided not to come back at all. I have a few things to collect for him, but there isn't much. I'll put it all into a box and take it with me as excess baggage.' All the time she was speaking, Rochelle's big blue eyes were fixed upon her with an odd expression, and when she had finished, she heard Rochelle say slowly and wonderingly, 'You've grown up, Jody. You seem most efficient, and to know exactly where you are going.'

'I must admit I've gained confidence. A little of it seemed to come as soon as I'd talked to Mr. Thorpe and realised I had a home and security. Then I seemed to gain more during those two days I was at the castle. Mr. Blake was so charming with me, and although he did regard me as a . . . well, a child, he also treated me as an equal, showing me everything, including the books, and advising me to have my own accountant to see to my affairs. It's plain that he and my great-uncle never had a cross word, and Mr. Blake seemed to think he ought to look after me . . . well, that was the impression I had.' Jody's eyes became dreamy and wide, and a lovely smile hov-ered on her lips. She was staring into space, thinking of the pleasure of being with Conor Blake, and so she missed the glint of cold steel that entered Rochelle's blue eyes and vanished a second before Jody looked at her again. 'He could easily have had someone else show me around the grounds,' she continued, 'but he took me himself. There's so much to see, Rochelle, you have no idea. And to think that half of it is mine.' She stopped and swallowed; speech had become too difficult for a few emotional seconds. 'It's like a miracle.'

'It is indeed.' Rochelle lifted her cup to sip her tea, her expression veiled. 'Tell me some more about this handsome partner of yours.'

'Mr. Blake!' Jody's eyes glowed. 'He's a very busy man, but he managed to spend quite a lot of time with me, telling me how the business started, and about the vast amount of renovating the castle had undergone at various stages of its history. It's no wonder it's one of the world's most famous hotels, because it's so beautiful and luxurious, and filled with exquisite carvings and antiques and paint-ings. . . .' Jody allowed her voice to trail off as she gave a wry grimace. 'I could go on for hours about it,' she added self-depreciatingly.

'I was asking about your partner.'

'Oh, yes.' Again Jody's eyes came alive, crystal clear and sparkling. 'Well, I have described him to you, and said how charming and considerate he was with me. I must admit that at first I was overawed by the magnificence of him, but later he seemed to go out of his way to put me at my ease. And when we dined in that romantic atmosphere, it was lovely! I wondered how I came to be there, with such a handsome gentleman, sitting at his private table in a corner by the big high window which looks out to the gardens and the Corrib; it was like a fairy tale!'

A silence followed, strange and intense, before it was broken by Rochelle, who, as if for something to say, asked about Old Bill. 'Mr. Blake did not object to having him around, then?' she added.

'No. As a matter of fact, they took to one another as soon as they met. Mr. Blake had one of the gardeners show him the cottage, and although it wasn't really ready for immediate occupation, having stood empty for a few weeks, it did have a little furniture in it, so Old Bill took his suitcase and moved in right away.' Jody said no more because she was afraid of embarrassing Rochelle by the reminder that she had intended to turn Old Bill out without anywhere to go.

'From what you've told me of Mr. Blake, I'd not have thought he'd want anyone like Old Bill around. He can scarcely add prestige to the place, just the contrary. And yet he's provided him with a cottage, you say?'

'That's right,' said Jody, ignoring the first two sentences. 'There are quite a number of cottages in the grounds, mainly tucked away behind what was once a deer park, and these cottages house some of the staff, mainly gardeners.'

'Gardeners,' murmured Rochelle to herself. 'I shan't even have a garden at all with my flat.'

'But you're looking forward to having it, surely? Otherwise you'd not have decided to sell this house and buy it.'

Rochelle shrugged and sighed. Her mind was not on the small flat at this moment, but on a beautiful castle standing in three hundred acres of glorious Irish countryside.

'It won't be ready yet awhile,' was all she said about the flat. 'This castle—as I mentioned, I'd love to see it. Shall I come over with you when you go? I could have a week's holiday there.'

'Oh, will you, Rochelle?' eagerly and with fresh hope for a deep bond coming into existence between them. 'I'd love that.'

'Then it's settled.' Rochelle's smile was winning and spontaneous. 'I must go out and buy myself a whole new wardrobe, seeing that I'm to stay in one of the most luxurious and famous hotels in the world.'

Undoubtedly Rochelle looked superbly elegant and beautiful, and Jody, who had been so happy previously when dining with Conor Blake, now felt dejected and inadequate, unable to join in the flow of conversation taking place between the two most distinguished-looking people among the hundred or so who were dining late in the candlelit restaurant of the hotel. Jody sighed and toyed with her food, miserably aware that neither of her companions had noticed her lack of appetite . . . or so she thought, sunk as she was in brooding self-pity because, having had Conor's full attention during her previous two-day visit, she had felt shut out almost from the moment she had introduced the two four days ago. It had seemed to Jody's critical eyes that Rochelle had instantly set out to captivate Conor, just as she always did captivate men. They swarmed about her like drones round the queen bee. But Rochelle had said from the first that she intended being selective.

'Money, looks and position—that's what I want and that's what I intend to get,' she had once said to Jody . . . and there was no doubt that Conor Blake possessed these three important requirements.

'Jody, you're not eating your fish.' Conor's voice, though gentle, was edged with authority, and Jody reflected on her initial impression that he felt he must take care of her until she was a little older.

'I'm not very hungry.'

Rochelle glanced at her and purred, 'You look rather pale, Jody, darling. Perhaps you ought to go to bed early. Don't you agree, Mr. Blake?'

He seemed concerned, but much to Jody's relief, he was not ready to agree with Rochelle's suggestion. 'Perhaps you'll enjoy the main course better,' he said with a smile. 'Certainly leave that if you don't want it.'

After that Jody's appetite miraculously revived, and as from then on Conor went out of his way to bring her into the conversation, the evening passed quite pleasantly after all.

Later, when Conor had said good night to them both and Jody was in her sitting room, Rochelle knocked and came in, then made herself comfortable, seating herself on the deep, softly cushioned sofa, crossing her elegantly clad legs after bringing up the skirt of her evening dress.

'You're not going to bed yet, are you?' she said, and Jody could not help recalling her earlier suggestion that Jody ought to be in bed.

'Well, I was going . . . in a minute or two.'

'I wanted to make a suggestion, Jody.'

'Yes?'

'I did say that my flat's not ready, didn't I? It needs things done to it which will take some time, so I thought I'd live here for a few weeks. This suite's large enough for two—'

'It has only the one bed,' cut in Jody hastily.

'Yes, but your bedroom's plenty big enough for two singles, isn't it?' That winning smile appeared,

44

and the big blue eyes were wide and frank and friendly. 'You'll need company, because there's nothing much for you to do here. Conor's explained that he alone manages this hotel, and it's obvious that he won't tolerate any interference from you. So what about my suggestion?' Again that disarming smile, that open friendly stare.

Jody bit her lip, fully aware that, only a few days ago, she would have welcomed Rochelle's suggestion, anxious to have the opportunity of cementing a friendship, but not now. Jody knew for sure that, should Rochelle come to live here, then she, Jody, would very soon have her nose pushed out altogether.

'I don't think you should come here—except for a holiday now and then. You've to see about your removal, too. I expect the mortgage is through by now, so those people will want possession of the house.'

'Of course they will, and that's why I'd like to stay here. I've nowhere to go when I move out of there.'

Nowhere to go. . . . How recently it had been that, when Jody had made a similar statement, Rochelle had declared it was none of her concern.

Firmly Jody said, looking straight at her, 'I'd rather you didn't stay here, Rochelle. I'm sorry, but it wouldn't work. I really don't need company, because I intend to see to such things as the flowers —and that's a big undertaking because there are so many rooms, to say nothing of the arrangements we put on every table in the restaurant.' Jody's eyes were towards the window and the view over the lovely lake with the dark silhouette of the mountains behind, their sharp peaks jutting into the starlit sky. So she did not notice the shades of anger that darkened Rochelle's eyes, or that her teeth had clamped together, bringing her mouth into an ugly line of compression.

'So you don't want me?'

Jody frowned without turning, and heard Rochelle add tightly, 'It's Conor, isn't it? You don't like the idea of his interest in me?'

'His interest?' Something slashed at Jody's heart-strings, and her breath came faster.

'It's obvious that he's attracted to me.' There was a confident, airy manner about Rochelle as she went on. 'He would be delighted for me to stay.'

'He . . . said so?' A nameless sense of misery assailed Jody, and with a little instinctive gesture she put a hand to her heart—for what reason, she could not understand. 'He said so?' she repeated when Rochelle hesitated.

'Yes, he said so,' answered Rochelle after another small pause. 'He finds me attractive, so naturally he wants me to stay.'

'How long?'

'A few weeks, until my flat is ready.'

Jody looked at her, sitting there as if the suite was hers, and Jody the intruder. A sudden anger flared within Jody, and all her newfound confidence came to the fore. There was dignity in her manner despite the pressure she was under.

'I don't care what my partner wants, Rochelle. It so happens that I don't think I'd like you to be here for any longer than the week you originally planned. So please consider my decision as final.' And with that she walked to the door and opened it. 'I'm tired, Rochelle, so please leave me. I'm sorry about my decision—'

'If you're sorry, then why make it?' gritted Rochelle, furious at the humiliation she was being made to suffer by the girl she had always despised. She was in effect being ordered out of her apartment, and a black venom of hatred rose like a burning vapour inside her.

'What I meant was,' said Jody, marvelling at the cool composure she was able to exhibit, 'that I regret having to make the decision.' With the door in her hand she looked at Rochelle as she rose from the sofa and began to cross the beautiful high-ceilinged room. "You must admit, you didn't really want me, Rochelle, not until I inherited half of this hotel.'

Rochelle's teeth snapped together. After a hostile pause she swept past Jody with a flurry of organza and lace, then turned in the corridor, her face pale with anger. 'I shall see Conor. The final decision will be his!'

It was to transpire that Rochelle did not speak to Conor after all, because when she and Jody were at the breakfast table the following morning, Jody was given the message that Conor had gone to his other hotel in Dublin and would not be back for about a week. Watching Rochelle's face, Jody saw her mouth droop and her eyes lose their lustre.

'You never told me about this other hotel,' was all Rochelle said when the girl bringing the message had moved away.

'I didn't know he owned one. He didn't mention anything to me about it.'

'I suppose there was no need, since it had nothing to do with you.' Jody made no comment; she was surprised to find she could eat a hearty breakfast of bacon and eggs garnished with sliced mushrooms and strips of delicious grilled kidney. Rochelle, on the other hand, seemed not to be hungry. 'Another hotel, and in Dublin,' Rochelle was murmuring. 'Conor Blake must be a millionaire several times over. I wonder how many hotels he owns altogether.'

'Aren't you eating anything?' inquired Jody, deliberately ignoring Rochelle's words. 'Your breakfast's getting cold.' Rochelle looked down at her plate, but her interest was not in food, Jody decided. No, it was fixed upon what was running through her mind: the extent of Conor Blake's wealth.

The next day Rochelle received a telephone call from the people who were buying her house. The mortgage had come through and they wanted to take possession as soon as possible after the settlement, which was imminent. So Rochelle left the castle on the day previously arranged, and Jody sincerely hoped she had seen the last of her, the hopes she had cherished of a closer relationship having been crushed by Rochelle's attitude towards her, and even more by her interest in Conor Blake.

Why this interest should trouble her so much, Jody did not know. She did know that she herself was affected by Conor Blake, inexpressibly happy when in his company, feeling safe and cared for—sort of, she mused as, having seen Rochelle into the taxi and dutifully stood on the castle steps to wave good-bye, she made her way across the wide lawns and through delightful formal gardens, past a graceful fountain where the crystal waters flaunted the rainbow colours they had taken from the sun. Behind the ancient deer park she found Old Bill weeding his own small garden and remembered that it was his day off.

'How are you doing, little Jody?' He was pleased to see her and instantly tossed down the trowel he had been using to stir up the soil between two neat rows of young lettuce plants. 'Sit down and I'll make you a cup of tea. How's Rochelle?'

'Gone back home.' Jody sat down on the little rustic seat which Old Bill had made for himself. Four Rhode Island Red hens scratched and clucked in a small netted enclosure not far away. 'You're getting nicely settled, Bill. Where did you get the hens?'

'Bought them from a farmer on the other side of Cong. They're all laying.'

'So you have your own eggs. And soon you'll have your own vegetables.' Her eyes strayed to the plot where the tops of carrots and turnips and onions could just be seen in regimented rows, all strong and likely to grow well. 'But don't you get vegetables given to you?'

'Of course. We all take what we want, but there's nothing like having a few growing outside one's back door.' His lined old face was creased in a smile. He was happy, really content and comfortable for the first time in his life. So long to wait . . . Jody's soft brown eyes were sad because she felt he had not a great deal of time in which to enjoy this new and interesting life he was now leading. He had a proper job, with excellent wages, and this pretty cottage to live in. 'Do you know, little Jody, that Rochelle never once came over to see me, and she was here for a week, you said?'

'That's right.'

A huskiness in her tone made the old man say, 'Something wrong, young Jody? You don't seem as cheerful as you usually are.' He was at the open door of his cottage, but he stood a moment, waiting for her answer.

'I'm all right,' she assured him.

But he looked at her perceptively and said, 'Rochelle. She's upset you. I did say you shouldn't have had her here, didn't I?'

'Yes, but by then it was too late. She already was here.'

'She persuaded you to let her come.'

'I didn't really need persuading,' Jody had to admit. 'You see, when she was so eager to come with me, I felt there might be some hope for us to be friends—'

'Then you're more naive than I thought,' broke in Old Bill rather crossly. 'You should have known that it was nothing more than curiosity that brought her here. She wanted to see what you've inherited, and I'll bet my last penny she's crazed with envy.' He looked at her and shook his head. 'You had already told her about Mr. Blake?'

'Naturally. She asked me all about the man who was now my partner.'

A sigh escaped him; he was nodding, his pale eyes narrowed and perceptive. 'You shouldn't have told her a single thing, young Jody. That one's bad, looking to her own ends all the time. There's some gossip that she was all over Mr. Blake, even running after him one day when he was walking in the garden, and asking him to show her round. She was trying to flirt with him, Tommy O'Donovan said— he's one of the younger gardeners and he wasn't taken with Rochelle at all. She was very arrogant with him one day, actually telling him he ought not to be weeding in front of the castle when the guests were about. He wasn't weeding, but digging out a bush that had been attacked by rot and was dying. He'd been told to do it by the head gardener, so he was only obeying orders. He said Rochelle acted as if it were she who owned half the place, not you.'

'Rochelle said that to him?' Jody's brown eyes blazed. 'How dare she! I wish I'd known.'

'Well, it's done with now, so not to worry. I'll go and make that tea.'

'Shall I help?'

'Come in and see my new chair. It's winged and very comfortable. I bought it in Cong only yesterday and they delivered it right away. Young Jody, it's great to have a bit of money in my pocket to spend as I want. Thank you,' he added huskily, just as if he had a lump in his throat, and ambled off, as if he wanted to hide his expression from her . . . or perhaps there was the hint of tears in those pale eyes, she thought, tenderness sweeping over her. Old Bill was still her dearest friend, the one she would come to if ever things went wrong . . . just as she had come to him today, the moment she had seen Rochelle into the taxi which had taken her away from the castle to the airport and then home.

"Your chair's lovely!" she called from her comfortable place on its soft upholstery. 'You'll be going to sleep in this!'

'You like it, then?'

'It's great!'

'I can get a sofa to match when I've worked another few weeks. I've already put a deposit on it and the man's saving it for me.' Old Bill was rattling crockery and Jody's eyes widened when he came from the kitchen with a tray on which were two bright beakers and matching sugar bowl and cream jug.

'What . . . ?'

'Like 'em?' He was obviously delighted by her surprise. 'Irish pottery. Tommy's wife got them for me when she went into Limerick to see her mother. She said it was an Irish custom to buy a new

51

neighbour a house-warming present, so she bought me this set, which also has two plates and two dessert bowls. I've never had anything like this lovely crockery in my whole life!' Old Bill led the way out to the garden, and Jody followed, the prick of tears behind her eyes.

'You make good tea,' she said absurdly, but she had to say something. They were sitting on the rustic bench and he had drawn up an old milking stool to house the tray.

'I'm going to save for a carpet next,' said Old Bill contentedly. 'I've never had a carpet, as you know. Tommy's wife's going to take me in the car to Limerick, where I can buy one fairly cheaply.'

'Can I buy it, for your birthday?'

'It'll be expensive for you, little Jody.'

She laughed then, a tinkling laugh that sounded like sheep bells in the meadow. 'You seem to forget that I'm rich.'

'Yes, I did for the moment. You used to save your pocket money, didn't you, to buy me birthday and Christmas presents? Well, if you really want to buy the carpet, I'll not say no, because I want to get some material for curtains for my bedroom. Tommy's wife's going to sew them for me.'

'Tommy and his wife sound nice. Where do they live?'

'Just across, in the trees. They've two little ones who come now and then for a chat.'

'That'll be company for you.'

'It is. I like little ones. . . .' His voice trailed off, the sigh issuing from his lips saying far more than words ever could have done.

'Is there anything else you're urgently in need of?' Jody asked before she left. She had wanted to buy him all new furniture for the cottage, but he had preferred to take over what little the previous tenant had left behind.

'I want to buy my own, and make the improvements as I go along,' he had said after apologetically refusing her offer. 'It'll be more fun that way, and give me a great deal of satisfaction.' And because Jody realised he was like a child with a new toy, she had left him to his own devices. 'No, thank you, little Jody, there's nothing I want urgently. Mr. Blake was saying something about a television set he has stored away at the castle, and he's having it looked over to see that it works all right, and then I can have it.'

'You're very happy, aren't you, Bill?' said Jody affectionately.

'Happier than I have ever been before.' He stood up and half-turned from her. 'Come again soon . . . and if that Rochelle writes and wants to come again, just you tell her she can't!'

'I will,' returned Jody, and meant it.

Chapter Four

Conor Blake arrived home two days before he was expected. Jody was stunned by the joyous leaping of her heart and the tremors of an emotion both new and faintly disturbing. She had known that he affected her in some strange, profound way which she could not have analysed even had she tried. But she did not try; it was enough that she felt safe with him, secure in the conviction that he would protect her— though from what, she had no notion. Sometimes these thoughts actually amused her, because they were fanciful, the rambling, unconnected dreams of a child.

She was in the Corrib Lounge, drinking an aperitif with one of the guests, a lady on her own who was writing a book on ancient abbeys in Ireland, which was the reason why she had come to Cong. Seeing her on her own, Jody had decided to join her, just to make her feel more at home. And she was so keenly interested in what the woman was saying that she did not at first realise that Conor had come into the lounge and was standing by the carved oak fireplace, chatting to a party of four Americans who had booked into the hotel that very day and were staying for two weeks.

Jody saw him at the same time he saw her, and they smiled. Her day was made, and even more so when presently he excused himself and came over to join her and Mrs. Grahame. He called for a drink, then the three chatted for a while, with Conor showing keen interest in Mrs. Grahame's project.

'I have several books on Cong,' he said after learning that she was staying at the hotel for at least a week. 'They're in my own private library but I shall be delighted to lend them to you if they will help in your research.'

Mrs. Grahame was delighted, and promised to take great care of the books.

'I'm so glad you got back early,' Jody was saying when, just about an hour later, she was sitting opposite him at the corner table, which was now as much hers as his. Conor had never suggested she should sit anywhere else for her meals. How very nice it was not to have Rochelle dominating the candlelit table with its flowers and gleaming cutlery and crystal glass, thought Jody, glad she had put on a long evening dress—a white organza creation she had bought when she and Rochelle had spent a day in Limerick. Rochelle had not liked the dress, but Jody had bought it all the same, along with dainty white sandals to match, and a small white silk rose for her hair. It was fun dressing up, which she could do every night if she wished, because most of the women wore long dresses for dinner, and the men were asked to wear jackets and ties. Conor looked superlatively well-dressed and masculine in an oyster-grey suit and pale blue shirt, his dark skin clear and shining, his hair with its sprinklings of grey immaculately brushed back from his wide forehead. So distinguished! Envious eyes were cast in Jody's direction by young women and old alike. Joy filled her heart every time Conor smiled at her, and only now did it strike her that very rarely had he been out of her thoughts since the moment she had first met him, just over four weeks ago.

'You've been lonely since Rochelle went home?'

'Not lonely, because I've found myself plenty to do. But it's very nice to have you back, Mr. Blake.' Her expressive brown eyes met his, and she heard his soft Irish brogue coming to her across the table as the wine waiter stood beside the cooler, ready to open the champagne which was standing in ice. Conor instructed him to come back later.

'I think it is time you began calling me Conor, don't you?' Conor seemed amused by the rush of colour that fused her cheeks.

She continued to look at him, though, as she said, a shy edge to her sweet young voice, 'I'd like that . . . Conor.' More colour flooded her cheeks; his laugh was indulgent, bringing a slight frown to Jody's brow, her feelings mixed because on the one hand she liked the idea of his being a sort of guardian, but she had recently realised that the last thing she wanted was for him to regard her as a child. Nor did she feel like one. Taking it for granted that one day she would be called upon to accept some responsibility in the running of the hotel, she had been watching and learning, especially since

Rochelle had left two days before. Her self-confidence was growing all the time, helped by the respectful attitude of the entire staff. Young as she was, they had accepted her, and whenever she rang down for anything to be brought up to her suite, she was attended to without the slightest delay. Not that she did send for anything now, but when Rochelle was at the castle she would often come to Jody's rooms and ask her to ring down for drinks or other refreshments.

'Have you looked at the menu?' Conor asked, breaking into her thoughts.

'No. It was brought to me in the lounge, but I was too interested in what Mrs. Grahame had to say. She's doing a whole chapter on Cong Abbey. Rochelle and I went to see it twice last week.'

'She's interested in things like that?'

Jody hesitated a moment and then said candidly, 'Not altogether. She came with me, though, and took some snapshots of the chancel and the Gothic doorways.'

'But she wasn't really interested, not like Mrs. Grahame?'

'No, but then, Mrs. Grahame's writing about it.'

Conor let that pass, becoming absorbed in the menu. Jody felt almost elated at the casual way he had spoken of Rochelle, for it seemed definitely to reveal his lack of interest in her as a woman.

'I can recommend the Zurich veal with mushrooms,' Conor said, his eyes still on the menu. 'It's done in white wine and served with a cream sauce and buttered noodles. You can have a mixed salad with it if you wish.' Lowering the menu, he looked at her, a half-smile on his lips.

Her eyes were glowing because of his interest in

her and the expression in his eyes, as if he were finding something to admire in her appearance. Jody was thrilled to be with him, yet dazed by it all—the splendour of the castle with its countless art treasures, the intimate and fairy-tale-like atmosphere of the dining room with its warm glowing lights, mainly from candles, and its incredibly lovely views of the regal approach to the hotel, the river which danced beneath the stone bridge, the ancient deer park, thickly wooded and mysterious in the light from a low moon impaled on the tip of a tall slender cypress standing sentinel-like against the star-sprinkled sky. For there was a strange aura about it all which made Jody think of those ancient times when kings ruled the wild tribes that occupied the whole length and breadth of what was then a barbaric land. And Conor Blake was descended from one of those tribes. . . . Smiling at her thoughts, she had no idea just how charmingly young and feminine she appeared to the man sitting opposite her, the experienced, mature man who had so unexpectedly found himself with a partner who was so much younger than he that from the first he had known a protective instinct towards her, convinced that this would have been what her great-uncle would have expected of him.

'Well,' he pressed, 'what are you having for your main course?'

'What you recommended,' she replied at once. 'And for dessert I'm having banana Lisette. I had it last week and it was delicious!'

'That's settled, then.' Lifting a hand casually, he brought a waiter to the table at once. The order given, he then chatted with Jody, telling her about Dublin and answering the many questions she kept on asking him. At last he said, 'I'm going again next week. How would you like to come with me? Dublin's a city you ought to see. It's very attractive.'

'"Dublin's fair city,"' she murmured, '"where the girls are so pretty."' And she laughed then and the glow in her devastatingly beautiful eyes caught and held her companion's attention for a long, profound moment before, with a slight frown that was totally unexpected, he flicked a hand to fetch the wine waiter and Jody had the impression that he was faintly angry over something and did not want to look at her on account of it. Realising she had not answered his question, she said swiftly, lest he should change his mind, 'I'd love to come to Dublin with you, Conor. Shall we stay in your hotel?'

'Of course. Where else should we stay?'

'Where is it? In the centre of the city?'

Conor nodded his head, his attention on the wine waiter, who was opening the champagne. 'Yes; it looks onto St. Stephen's Green Park in a tree-lined road. I think you'll like it.'

'What's the name of it?'

'The Greenwood.' Jody thought of Rochelle and her curiosity as to how many more hotels Conor owned, and after a small hesitation she said, 'Have you any more, Conor?'

'Yes, two. One in Cork and one in Waterford.'

Jody's eyes widened. 'Four hotels!' she exclaimed. 'You must work very hard.'

'Three and a half hotels.' Conor gave her a faint smile, amusement in his dark metallic eyes. "No, I don't have to work very hard. I've three excellent managers to run the other hotels.'

'But you visit them now and then?'

'Of course, just to see how things are going.'

'Rochelle would have been interested . . .' Jody stopped, wondering how she had come to say a thing like that.

'Rochelle?' with a puzzled look. "What do you mean?'

'Oh . . . er . . . nothing,' she began, when he interrupted her, insistence in his soft Irish voice.

'You didn't say a thing like that for nothing, Jody. You had better explain.'

Jody frowned inwardly, cursing herself for the slip that had made her speak her thoughts aloud. Conor's face was stern, his eyes clearly demanding an answer to his question. Jody shrugged her shoulders, shaking off her reluctance because she knew prevarication would only be a waste of time. 'Rochelle was wondering how many hotels you owned—it was because we'd learned that you owned one in Dublin.'

'I had no idea Rochelle was so interested in my affairs.'

Curt the tone suddenly, and unable to prevent herself, Jody said, 'Do . . . do you like Rochelle?'

'Like her?' The soft inscrutable voice matched the unreadable mask of his face.

Jody moved uneasily, embarrassed by the coolness that seemed to have fallen between them. She ought not to have mentioned Rochelle, but it was done now, and she said quietly, 'I had the impression that you found her . . . well . . . attractive.'

A hush fell, but a moment that could have been awkward was relieved by the wine waiter pouring the champagne.

'I should imagine,' submitted Conor impassively at length, 'that most men find your adoptive sister attractive.'

Not a direct answer, and Jody quite naturally

wondered if there was some reason for it, and again words came which she was unable to force back. 'She said you'd be glad for her to stay longer.'

'She . . .' Amazement registering in those dark eyes told Jody all she needed to know even before he said, 'You must be mistaken, Jody. Rochelle could not have told you anything of the kind.'

'I'm beginning to think I was mistaken,' Jody lied, too exhilarated by what she had just learned to want to prolong the subject. And on reflection, she knew she ought to have doubted Rochelle's statement simply owing to the several hesitations she had made prior to its being voiced.

Jody hoped Conor would let the matter drop, and he did, the conversation becoming light and general. When the meal was over, they left the dining room, warm and soft with candlelight, to go into the Corrib Lounge, and Jody, who had tasted a liqueur for the first time only a month ago, readily accepted when Conor asked her if she would care for one with her coffee.

As it was only a quarter to ten when they had finished, Conor asked Jody if she would care to take a stroll with him in the grounds of the castle. Her heart jerked against its anchor and her eyes lit with a vibrant beauty that could not possibly escape Conor's attention. His own eyes became dark and sensual as they looked down into hers, and for Jody the silence was all-enveloping, with no one in the room but the two of them—her and the man of whose magnetism she was becoming increasingly aware.

'I'd . . . I'd love a walk,' she managed, rather breathlessly because of the sudden stirring of emotions which created a mingling of pleasure and excitement, with bewilderment hovering on the edge of her mind as she tried to discover a reason for the way she was feeling.

They crossed the great stone bridge to wander along the banks of the Cong River, where everything was silent and still except the shining waters and the gentle swaying of the tall pines against a sky sprinkled with a million crystal points of light. Time seemed to stand still for Jody, who yet again wondered how she came to be here in this unreal world of legendary beauty, of dignity and elegance reminiscent of a bygone age.

A tiny sigh of contentment escaped her, which was heard by her companion.

'What was that for, Jody?' His voice was soft, and she thrilled to its Irish intonation.

'It's all so peaceful and serene—another world . . .' She broke off to look up at his profile, strong and clear-cut in the moonlight, and knew a primitive urge to make physical contact with him—if only to touch his hand, that strong brown hand so close to her side.

'You've not been used to the country?'

She shook her head, thinking of the tall Victorian house, gracious, yes, but in a long row where many of its neighbours had been turned into flats, housing several families because a town was close, a busy town to which thousands of people rushed each morning to be imprisoned for the day behind counters, workbenches or desks. And something like that would have been her lot but for this incredible inheritance which had assured her comfort for the rest of her life.

'No, it's no longer country, but it was once, many years ago before Darcombe expanded.'

'You like the country?'

'I've always liked it, but here . . .' She gave a deep

contented sigh. 'Here it is different from anything I had ever imagined. Yours is a beautiful country, Conor.'

A slow smile lifted the corners of his mouth. 'I think so,' he said, slanting her a glance, noticing the silken halo of her hair, the delicate outline of her face. 'I'm glad you like it, Jody, because it is your country, too, you know. Your grandmother was true-bred Irish from Cork.'

'Yes, I always knew there was Irish blood in me, but I had no idea I was related to a wealthy man who would leave me his share in a wonderful hotel like this.'

'In all fairness, he owed it to you, or rather, your mother. You see, he had a fortune besides, but it all went to charities. He was interested in numerous charities—in fact, I often used to think he lived for them.'

'He must have been a very good man.'

'One of the best.'

'You miss him?'

'I miss his company, yes. I used to go to his suite and play chess with him. He didn't get about much at all towards the end,' Conor reminisced, then fell silent, and Jody refrained from disturbing his thoughts because she knew they were private and he would not want them to be interrupted. So they strolled along the riverbank in silence, the night warm and soft, with the river bright and shining on one side and the moon-splashed woodlands on the other, while in the star-studded distance the mountains of Connemara rose pure and positive against an argent light, wild creations of nature and the relentless ravages of wind and rain and ice over countless ages of time.

Unreal and lovely, with no one in the whole world

but her and the tall man at her side, his body lithe and lean, his chiselled features noble and stern and misleadingly arrogant—or was she wrong on that particular point? The fact that he had never shown arrogance towards *her* did not signify that he could not show it to someone else.

He came out of his detached mood and smiled into her upturned face. 'I think we ought to turn back,' he said. 'We'll take one of the little paths through the woods. You've probably realised that there are a number of these paths? They form a sort of nature trail.'

'Yes, but I haven't really explored them.'

Silence fell again, to be broken only when Jody, having caught her foot in a surface root, cried out as she instinctively made a grab at Conor's coat to save herself from falling.

'Oh . . . I'm sorry!' It had been an instinctive gesture, but even as she made to draw away, she felt the strength of Conor's arms about her, drawing her close to his body; the contact of his hand beneath her chin tilting her face was a nerve-spinning experience that shot tremors of pleasure through her body. For a long intense moment they looked at one another, Conor from his incredible height, Jody with her face firmly held . . . and then his dark head was bending. . . .

His first kiss was gentle, staggering them both, and it was brief. But his cool clean breath had stirred Jody's senses in some mystifying way, clouding her mind against rational thought. It was a moment of revelation and confusion when she was so deeply affected by the contact of a man's hard body, by the restrained but sensual touch of a man's lips on her own, that she seemed to be carried on a tide of wild abandon which fused her body closer while her hands slid along the silky whiteness of his shirt until they met behind his head. Her face, warm with the flush of breathlessness and expectation, was lifted to his, her eyes unblinking, her softly parted lips moist and shining, a sort of sacrificial invitation which for a moment seemed to take him completely by surprise.

He looked down from his great height, his scrutiny long and dark and unfathomable. And then his arms were crushingly strong about her, his mouth hard and dominating, ruthless in its demands. Awakened and appalled, with panic striking her senses, Jody tried to struggle, pushing her small white hands against the hard muscles of his chest, but she was helpless in the prison of his arms, and when his lips came down on hers for the third time, new emotions surged within her so that she willingly reciprocated, obeying his arrogant demand, bending to his sensual domination. Wild, bewildering desires swept away any instinct except the primitive one of submission and fierce participation. She quivered as his hand caressed her white throat, moving gently to her shoulder, down her bare arm, feather-light, but tempting enough to spur her reflexes, and again she tried to free herself. But it was a halfhearted attempt, and even so, she stood little chance of escape against the increased pressure of the hand holding her to him, or the insistence of the other as it slid round her and she felt his fingers hard against the small of her back. Ecstasy fired her senses as his mouth found hers yet again; she thrilled to the masterful insistence of hard possessive lips forcing hers apart, and rapture drenched her body at the contact of a man's tongue with hers.

At last he held her away from him, at arm's

length, and looked down at her flushed face before his eyes flickered to her heaving breasts, pulsating with life beneath the tight-fitting bodice of her dress.

'You're a very lovely child,' he murmured, but shook his head, and she knew that already he was regretting what he would consider a lapse. A nameless feeling of shame and humiliation went side by side with a feeling of hopeless misery because she felt he would never succumb to such weakness again. 'Come,' he urged, a gentle hand beneath her elbow. 'It's getting late; you ought to be in bed.'

'It . . . it . . . wasn't wrong . . .' She lifted protesting eyes, her lashes stiff and moist. 'Are you sorry, Conor, for . . . for k-kissing me?'

'Certainly I am!' he almost snapped. 'It was totally unforgivable of me. Try to forget it! It won't happen again!'

Chapter Five

A very lovely child. . . . Those words swam about in Jody's brain long after she had gone to bed. She had known, of course, the light in which her partner regarded her. Yes, she was a mere child, the great-niece of a man he had deeply admired, who had been his friend, and his father's before him. Austin O'Rourke would have liked to think that Conor was taking care of the girl to whom he had left his share of the hotel. So Conor had accepted it as a duty that he would look after her, protect her. Yet he had had a lapse and kissed her. . . . And now he was angry and repentant, declaring it was unforgivable of him to have done it.

Jody's shame and humiliation and misery merged into one all-oppressive feeling of loss and an emptiness within her which as the hours passed she began to resent quite bitterly because until the incident she had been so happy, so delighted with the change in her circumstances, so secure. . . .

But now that security seemed to be in the balance, as if it could be taken from her. And it was only as this registered that she realised that security lay in her relationship with Conor rather than the dramatic change in her financial position. Conor was her prop; he spelled safety, not the inheritance. If anything should happen to weaken their relationship, then she knew she would feel as if all support had been snatched from her.

She wondered how he would behave when she met him at lunchtime. Perhaps he would avoid her, she thought unhappily, but no—he was there at the table when she entered the restaurant. A smile appeared, as if he would put her at her ease, and she smiled back; her world was rosy again. He had stood up as she reached the table, and it was he who came round to pull out her chair. She felt the contact of his jacket against her arm, caught his breath, warm and clean, and the smell of after-shave, which she liked. She wondered if he could smell her perfume; it was an expensive French brand, a great extravagance which was brought back to her each time she used it. Rochelle had had some once, bought by Philip as a thank-you present for the way Rochelle had worked at his books. Jody had asked if she could try it, just once, but Rochelle had said no. Perfume was worn for men, and so it was a waste for Jody to wear it.

'What have you been doing with yourself this morning?' inquired Conor as he sat down again.

'I've been doing the flowers. I've a few more to do yet. It's a lovely task. . . ." She was seized with shyness because of last night and the way she had so eagerly reciprocated his kisses.

'And you do them very well,' he praised. 'I don't

suppose the florist in Cong is very happy about your taking over his work.'

'They used to send someone up to do the flowers?'

'Of course.'

'I'm sorry. . . .'

'There's no need to be. We grow a multitude of flowers in the greenhouses, so they ought to be used.'

Jody said nothing. She was looking at him and thinking that as far as he was concerned, the incident which had so greatly troubled her might not have happened. If it was not forgotten altogether, it was certainly packed away in some remote corner of his mind.

'What have *you* been doing?' she asked at length.

'As usual, I've been working in my study.'

'I should have thought you'd have a secretary.'

'I did have until recently. She left to join her fiancé, who had previously gone out to Australia. That was six weeks ago, and I haven't replaced her yet.'

'But you will?'

'I shall have to.' Conor became thoughtful. 'Yes, I shall have to get a secretary soon.'

Again Jody fell silent, her mind wandering. And then with a little sense of shock it was borne in on her that she was hoping Conor's new secretary would be middle-aged and married.

Once again it was Old Bill's day off, and as soon as Jody had finished her self-imposed task of arranging the flowers for the dinner tables, she went off to spend an hour with him. He was in his garden, just standing there admiring a neat little plot of newly turned earth. The soil had been raked down so finely that Jody could not see one small lump anywhere.

'Admiring your handiwork, Bill?' Her smile was reflected in her eyes as she came up to him, waving a hand to indicate the plot.

'There's something about newly dug and raked earth,' he said slowly. 'I've been getting it ready for some cabbage seedlings I was given yesterday by Paddy.'

'He's given you lots of lovely things for your garden, hasn't he?' Paddy was the head gardener at Rushwood, and right from the start he had taken to Old Bill.

'He's very generous to us all.' As Old Bill turned to look at her, his eyes brightened. 'The carpet came yesterday, too, and Tommy was over last night to help me lay it. Come on in and see.' He was as excited as a young bride setting up home for the first time. 'Lisa, Tommy's wife, had made the curtains, and she came and fixed them for me.' He led the way, his step lighter than she had ever known it when he worked for her father.

'You seem years younger,' she remarked, noticing too that he was now taking more trouble with his appearance. His hair was clean and he had it cut; his shirt was clean, too, but he still wore the shoes with the holes in the toes.

'Oh, but this is an incredible transformation!' she exclaimed, stopping at the door of the living room to stare with widening eyes. He had chosen a red carpet, and the drapes were flowered, with brilliant red peonies predominating. The winged armchair was facing the television; the fireplace with its brass andirons was neatly laid with paper and sticks and to one side lay a stack of neatly cut logs. Through one small window the afternoon sun sent shafts of mellow light, showering the pretty little room with warmth. 'It's lovely, Bill! You must be feeling like a dog with two tails!'

'A millionaire,' he corrected, and suddenly his voice was tender. 'It's all due to you, little Jody.' He turned his head away from her, and she knew he was too full to say more.

'You're very lucky with your neighbours,' she commented, walking into the room. 'Lisa has made a very good job of these curtains.'

'Yes, I think so. And now I'm intending to start on my bedroom . . .' He broke off, and a wry smile tilted the pale dry lips. 'Come and see, so that you can compare when I've done it up.'

'It's awful!' Jody followed him into the other room. 'Why don't you let me help, Bill?'

'I'd rather do it, love. It's the first time in my whole life I've had a place of my own, and I want to feel the pride of doing it all myself. There's something you can't explain about building a home, isn't there?'

She nodded, a little lump rising in her throat at the idea of anyone who had worked as hard as Old Bill reaching the age of seventy-six before being able to make a home of his own. Still, he had it now, and all she hoped and prayed was that he would live to enjoy it for many years to come. Certainly he seemed very young for his age these days, and she put it all down to this new interest, this carrying out of plans which, as yet, had gone without a single hitch. What he wanted, he seemed determined to have.

'Are you going to paper the walls in here, Bill?' she inquired, glancing around.

'I'd like to, but this room's a bit damp, and Tommy says paper might not stick.'

'Damp? You can't sleep in a damp room, Bill,' she said concernedly.

'I've slept in fields,' he told her, laughing. 'Now, don't you go worrying yourself about me and a bit of damp!'

She came away, out into the brightness of the little sun patio which, she noticed, he had embellished with a few flowering plants and trailing ivies. There were two striped canvas garden chairs, faded by the sun but looking very comfortable to sit in.

'Did Tommy give you these chairs?' she wanted to know.

'They were in one of the dungeons—'

'Dungeons?' she blinked. 'Where are they?' There was a 'Dungeon Bar' in the hotel, of course, named mainly for the American guests who loved such things because they were ancient and intriguing. 'We have no real dungeons here, Bill—not those horrible places where they used to torture people. Rush-wood's a happy castle with no really gruesome history that I know of.'

'There are dark places beneath,' he said. 'I suppose they are really only cellars, though. I found the chairs, and Paddy said I could have them. Like them?' he asked proudly.

Jody sat down. 'This one's most comfortable.' She leant back and Bill went off to make a pot of tea. How little were his needs for perfect happiness, she mused. But then, all was relative; he had had practically nothing, and now he had something, and this time it was all his very own.

That evening she dined as usual with Conor, and very soon she was talking about Old Bill and mentioning the damp in the bedroom.

'I don't want him to get rheumatism'—she

frowned—'and so we must do something. What do you suggest, Conor?'

'Most of the cottages are a little damp,' he said. 'In the days when they were put up, the builders didn't include damp courses.'

'Can one be put in now for Old Bill?'

'Is it so very urgent?' A smile played about his mouth, and in his eyes there lay a sort of amused tolerance. A sigh touched her heart. She was trying hard to be more grown-up, to be assertive to a degree in the hope that Conor would begin to regard her less as a child and more as his partner in the business.

'It's urgent, yes, Conor. Old Bill is seventy-six and very well at present. It would be a shame if anything went wrong with his health, just when he is so happy.'

To her surprise, Conor said, in that attractive Irish voice of his, 'Tell me more about Bill. When I said he could have that old television set, he was like an excited youngster waiting to be given a very special birthday present.' Amusement in the tone, but mingling with it a curiosity, an interest that was genuine. A thrill of pleasure shot through Jody, and for a moment she just stared at him across the table, the candlelight bringing out the limpid quality of her eyes. She was wearing an evening blouse of bamboo green, high-necked and edged with gathered lace. The bodice was tight, accentuating her curves, the sleeves long with tight cuffs edged with lace to match that at her smooth white throat.

She told him about Bill—his early background and his trials and difficulties since. 'I was determined to bring him here,' she continued, contentedly aware that Conor's interest was still being held. 'He always said he had fallen on his feet when he came to work for my father, but looking back now, I see that he had very little in the way of comfort. He had a roof and good food, and that was about all.'

'And what has he here?' Conor's lean aristocratic face still showed interest; his very dark grey eyes were fixed on Jody's face.

'He has a home, Conor, and that is very different from a roof. He's made the living room beautiful—you have no idea! I never thought Old Bill had such excellent taste and imagination.' She paused a moment before voicing her next words. 'Why don't you go over and take a look?' she said. 'Old Bill would be thrilled to have you as his guest.'

Conor laughed then, and Jody caught her breath. What an incredibly handsome man he was! She liked everything about him—everything. . . . Suddenly her heartbeats were out of control and she found herself fumbling with an intangible yearning, felt herself to be groping through a mist where the light was tantalisingly out of her vision.

'You speak as though your friend would consider it an honour for him to have me as his guest. But that is not so, Jody, my dear. I am no better than Old Bill, just more fortunate, that's all.'

A deep sigh escaped Jody. What a wonderful philosophy Conor had; it was no wonder she loved him. . . . *Loved?* Stunned, she tried to marshal her thoughts, the colour mounting to her cheeks. So very naturally the truth had come to her, drifting into her consciousness as the aftermath of another thought: that Conor was a wonderful person.

So soon to fall in love with her partner! And he looked upon her as a child whom he must protect, not only because of her youth but because of the close relationship that had existed between her great-uncle and himself.

To her relief, Conor was talking to the wine waiter; they were discussing the merits of a new dry white they had recently added to their already extensive list. Jody willed the heat to recede from her cheeks, for Conor with his shrewd mind would instantly know that something was amiss. Jody had no wish to be asked what was wrong with her!

When at length the wine waiter moved away and Conor returned his attention to Jody, she had regained her composure to a great extent and said, 'About this damp in Old Bill's cottage—can a damp course be put in, even though the house is already built?'

'I think so, but it's expensive.' He looked intently at her as he said this, but she knew without any doubt at all that he would not mind the expense.

'You're willing to have it done, though?'

'Of course—if you are.'

'Me?' she queried, puzzled.

'Well, my dear, half the cost will be yours.'

'Oh, yes. I forgot I was a partner!'

'You're no businesswoman, that's for sure.' A small sigh seemed to escape him, and Jody found herself reluctantly thinking about Rochelle and her business acumen, the brilliant way she had kept their father's books from the time when she was little more than sixteen years of age. She would have made a far more acceptable partner to Conor, Jody thought, and wished she had more confidence in herself. But as her biology teacher had been used to saying, it was the gene machine that determined what a person was.

'I might improve with age,' she found herself saying, and at that they both laughed.

'So we arrange for your friend to have a damp course put into his cottage,' Conor said, changing the subject. 'You do realise that we are in duty bound to have damp courses put into all the other cottages?'

'Er . . . yes. You won't mind, will you, Conor? After all, it will improve the properties.'

He didn't mind at all, nor did he waste any time in contacting a builder who was willing to carry out the work.

'I don't really want a builder messing about with my house,' grumbled Old Bill when Jody went over to explain what was planned. 'They're clumsy, and they upset everything. What's a bit of damp, anyway?'

'You said you'd like paper on your wall . . .' began Jody, then stopped as he shook his head.

'I can paint it.'

'Well, it wouldn't look half as nice as paper. Besides, I'm worried about your health. You don't want to have rheumatism, do you?'

'Me, have rheumatics!' Bill laughed at the very idea. 'People like me never suffer from ailments of that kind! It's good of you, little Jody, to worry about me, but I shall take no harm.'

'It's all being arranged,' she told him firmly. 'The damp course is being put in, and that's the end of it. . . .' Her voice trailed off, and a smile lit her face as Tommy came along the little path leading to the front gate of the cottage garden.

'Hope I'm not intruding,' he said, lifting the latch. 'Miss Hendrick, is it true that we're all having damp courses put into our cottages?'

She nodded, sliding a glance towards Old Bill, who was still plainly disgruntled and making no attempt to hide the fact.

'Yes, that's right. What do you think of the idea?'

'Excellent. We have a little damp, just as Bill here has, and it'll be great to get it fixed.'

'Well?' Jody had turned to Old Bill, gesturing triumphantly. 'Do you feel better about it now?'

'Has he been complaining?' Tommy's laugh revealed his knowledge of Old Bill's character. 'The trouble with you, Bill, is that you've got yourself into a rut—and in no time at all! You want your house to be nice and dry, don't you?'

'I expect so,' muttered the old man resignedly. 'It's just that builders will make the devil of a mess.'

'We'll help you to clean it up,' promised Tommy, grinning at Jody. 'Your garden'll not suffer, if that's what's worrying you.'

'Oh, yes it will! What about those climbing roses I've put in by the front door, and the Virginia creeper by this window here?'

'They'll have to move those, I must admit, but you can soon plant some more.'

Bill said nothing, but his sigh could be heard, loud and protesting, even though he was obviously resigned and also of the opinion that he would be more comfortable once his house was made dry.

Three days later Conor said he was going to Dublin, and as Jody had by now convinced herself that he would have changed his mind about taking her with him, it was with a little shock of pleasure that she heard him say, 'If you want to come with me, you can.'

'I . . . ?' Her eyes widened with excitement. 'Yes, of course I want to come!' The eagerness with which she accepted his offer brought a slight frown to his brow, and she had the nagging little conviction that, could he have put back the clock for half a minute, he would not have extended the invitation. However, he had extended it, and she did not expect him to change his mind. 'How long shall we be away?'

'For three nights, that's all. I have several things I want to do.' He glanced at what she was wearing. 'You'll find some very attractive shops in Dublin, so go prepared to treat yourself.'

She smiled happily, saying it was lovely to have money to spend. 'It's still like a dream,' she ended, and was gratified to see him smile. 'When are we going?'

'On Wednesday.'

What should she pack? was Jody's next inquiry, and Conor told her to pack a couple of long dresses if she wished, but that they weren't really necessary.

'The Greenwood Hotel is very plush, but unfortunately, evening dress seems to be out of favour at the present time. Dublin women must be among the smartest in the world, but even they have no desire to dress for dinner. A few do, and you won't feel out of place in a long dress, but as I say, you needn't feel obliged to take any.'

Jody decided to compromise and take the two cocktail dresses she had bought in Limerick. One was a white cashmere, the other a fine cotton, embroidered at the waist and on the hem. Both were very chic—just right for going away, she thought, glad she had not yet worn either of them. Excitement was running high by the time Wednesday arrived, and it was impossible to hide it. Conor frowned on noting her flushed face, and again she felt sure he would not have invited her to accompany him had he the chance to do it over again.

They travelled in his Jaguar, at a speed that caused her to grip the seat beneath her knees. However, the Irish roads were not built for speeding over any great distances, and soon they were rolling along at a much more moderate pace. Jody was agog to see everything; the scenery often made her gasp with appreciation. The Emerald Isle . . . Yes, indeed, Ireland was green—so beautiful and green it seemed unreal in parts, just a lovely scene from a Walt Disney fantasy.

'I adore it!' she breathed. 'Where else in the world would you find such scenery as this?'

'I agree it's something special.' He paused a moment; then: 'But we do have a good deal of rain, you know. It takes a lot of water to produce all this lush vegetation.'

'And these sparkling cascades.'

'And the smooth rivers.'

It was late afternoon when they reached Dublin, a bustling city of parks and spires, of elegant Georgian houses rubbing shoulders with the usual concrete monstrosities seen rearing their ugly heads above most modern cities. What a pity, mused Jody, that man had lost the art of creating beautiful buildings. She looked about her as Conor snail-paced along Grafton Street, where cars were parked illegally, some actually on the pavement. Girls were laughing as they sauntered along, clothes chic and bright, hair shining. The men—the executive-set, especially— looked more serious in their formal suits, slim cases at their sides, faces tensed and faraway, as if their owners were burdened with all the worries of the world. Carefully negotiating both pedestrians and vehicles, Conor turned right into Nassau Street and then right again into Dawson Street. Ahead now was a barrier of foliage between the tall buildings left and right. As he swung into St. Stephen's Green, the sun emerged from behind a cloud and the trees in the park became golden. Jody continued to look about her. Road repairs, taxi ranks, innumerable cars, vans and lorries parked with careless abandon—all these combined to produce chaos which no one seemed able or willing to control.

'This is ridiculous!' exclaimed Jody on seeing a line of cars parked two abreast in an area where they should not have been parked at all. 'Where are the wardens?'

'Around somewhere,' was the casual response. 'You have to learn to live with this if you work in the city.' He pulled up at the front of an hotel facing the park. 'We're here,' he said, and a few moments later he was handing the keys to a porter so that he could take the car round to the hotel's private garage.

Jody looked round as she entered the lobby. Although lacking all the luxurious distinction of Rushwood Castle, the Greenwood wore an air of elegance and quiet refinement which Jody guessed at once would appeal to the businessman who wanted relaxation after a tiring day negotiating some deal in the city.

She mentioned the comparison and heard Conor say, 'Rushwood is for leisure, the Greenwood for convenience. We cater for the business executive and, of course, to those tourists who stay here for one night while on tour.'

The receptionist nodded and smiled as Conor walked past, Jody following closely. He had told her he had a suite set aside, and on entering it, she gave a little gasp. The sitting room was furnished with antique furniture; there was a thick wall-to-wall carpet and rich velvet drapes to match. A comfortable sofa and easy chairs were set before a mahogany fireplace and an office chair behind a lovely Georgian desk. There were two bedrooms, one with a circular double bed which Conor said Jody could have, along with the *en suite* bathroom whose sunken bath was the same shape and size as the bed. The other bedroom was smaller but also luxurious, with a bathroom *en suite*.

'This is lovely!' Jody walked all over the suite, which was in effect a large luxury penthouse occupying part of the top floor of the hotel.

That evening she and Conor dined privately in their suite. It was a cosy, intimate meal and they lingered over it until, on noticing Jody yawn several times, Conor said it was time she went to bed.

'Yes. . . .' She yawned again and got up from the table. This was another unreal experience, she mused, for here she was, sharing a suite with Conor . . . just as if he were her husband—except that she was to be alone in that massive bed while he occupied the smaller one right at the other end of the apartment. . . .

The following morning Jody said she would wander round the city while Conor went off to see his business associates.

'Don't get lost,' he said with a smile. 'I shall meet you back here at around five this afternoon.'

Jody went first to the fashionable shops in Grafton Street, then wandered down O'Connell Street. She found a select boutique and bought a fine tweed suit and a dress. Then she spent an hour in the museum before finding a little café just off St. Stephen's Green where she could buy a snack lunch. It was busy, and she found herself sharing a table with a very good-looking young man with a ready smile and a voice equally as attractive as Conor's.

'You on holiday?' he asked after hearing her give her order.

'No, I live in Ireland.'

'Here in Dublin?' He leant back in his chair and glanced around for the waitress.

'No, I live near Cong—over on the west in County Mayo.' As his eyes had been widening in surprise, Jody looked questioningly at him as she stopped speaking.

'Cong! Well, small world. I live in the village of Cong itself!'

'You do?'

'Yes. I'm over here for a few days' break. I've had my main holiday—went to London to visit relatives —but as I'd almost a week left, I decided to come over to the big city.' He laughed at that, and Jody knew why. There were no really big cities in Ireland.

'When are you going back?' she inquired conversationally.

'Probably tomorrow, or the next day at the latest.' His blue eyes examined her face with interest. 'How came you to be living in Ireland?'

She hesitated, then said with a smile, 'I inherited a half-share in an hotel and decided to come and live here permanently.'

'An hotel—near Cong?' There was a look of sudden perception in his vivid blue eyes.

'Rushwood Castle Hotel,' submitted Jody, and saw him begin to nod his head.

'So you're the English girl who inherited Austin O'Rourke's half of the Rushwood Castle Hotel.'

'You've heard of me, then?'

He grinned deprecatingly. 'Everybody has. Cong's a small village where everyone knows everyone else—and their business,' he added, eyes twinkling. 'Yes, we've all heard about you and said how lucky you are.'

'I think so too,' she said, smiling.

'How do you get along with your partner—or

shouldn't I ask that?' His gaze was fixed and appraising. 'You're a very attractive young lady,' he added for no reason at all, or so it seemed to Jody.

'We agree very well. Conor . . . Mr. Blake's an exceedingly nice gentleman.'

'So I believe.'

'You've never met him?' Jody looked surprised, knowing that at certain times of the year the restaurant was available to nonresidents. 'You've never dined at Rushwood?'

'Yes, I've dined there, but never seen Mr. Blake.' The waitress came to the table, notebook and pencil in her hands. 'I'll have an omelette and french fries,' he said.

'The usual.' She smiled at him and disappeared.

'You come in here every day?'

'It's cheap.' He looked amused as he added, ''I shouldn't have thought a young lady of your great wealth would patronise a café like this.'

'I only wanted a snack.' She studied him covertly as he beckoned to a young man who was serving glasses of house wine. Clear skin and a healthy colour in his cheeks, the look of the Irish—tough and enduring. His hair was lightish brown with fairer tints, his eyes the clearest blue she had ever seen. She guessed his age at about twenty-five and his height at just a little above average. A pleasant, reliable young man, she thought, one you could trust and who would protect you if need be. She smiled to herself, amused by her thoughts. Why was she assessing him like this? she wondered.

'How are you liking living here?' he asked. 'The west of Ireland's cold and wet for a large part of the year.'

'It's been warm and sunny since I've been there. I love it,' she added, answering his question. 'The scenery and the quietness. You never ever hear any traffic up there in the castle grounds.'

'It's beautiful, I admit.' He paused a second; then: 'My name's Turlough. It's a very ancient Irish name mainly used by the O'Neills and the O'Donnells. I'm Turlough O'Neill.'

'I'm Jody,' she submitted, shy all at once and wondering how she came to be talking to this young man as if she had known him for months instead of minutes.

'That's a pretty name. Can I use it?'

She paused fractionally before saying yes, he could use it.

Chapter Six

They sat in the park watching the water birds preening themselves on the sunny bank of the lake. Jody, stealing a glance at her companion's profile, wondered how she had come to let herself be persuaded to fall in with his suggestion that they walk around the park. She had spent more than an hour with him since leaving the café, and now they were sitting in companionable silence, after having talked and confided as they strolled along the shady paths between the bushes and trees. She had given him a brief résumé of her early life with her adoptive parents and sister and he had told her about his parents and his eight brothers and sisters, two of whom were still at home—Carmel and Tria, the latter only thirteen years old and determined to become a nun. Jody had told him about Old Bill, while Turlough had told her about his 'ancient uncle' who was once a tinker—in England called a gipsy—

but who had now been persuaded to make his home with Turlough's parents.

'But he flatly refuses to live in a house,' Turlough had continued ruefully. 'He insisted on a caravan, so Father bought him a new one and it's sited on a plot at the bottom of our garden.'

'Your uncle and Old Bill seem to be two of a kind,' Jody had said with a laugh.

'We ought to arrange a meeting,' was Turlough's immediate suggestion, but on thinking about it, Jody said noncommittally, 'Bill works on the Rushwood estate and in his spare time he looks after his own bit of garden. He's also getting his cottage in order, so I don't think he has time for much else.'

'Well, we shall have to see.' The conversation changed then, and gradually petered out altogether. By common consent they made for the bench and sat down, each immediately becoming absorbed in thought. Time sped by, and when Jody glanced at her watch, she gave a start of surprise.

'I must be going, Turlough. It's four o'clock and I want to get back and have a clean-up before Conor arrives at five.'

'It's been a most pleasant few hours,' he said.

'Yes, I've enjoyed it too.'

'I expect we shall bump into one another now and then in Cong.'

'I don't go into the village much.'

'I'll give you my telephone number. . . .' He had brought out a pencil and was searching in his pockets for a piece of paper. Jody produced a small diary from her handbag and opened it at the back.

'In there,' she said, pointing.

'If ever you want anything, or need help of any kind, then just ring me.' He handed the book back to her, and for a brief space her eyes remained on the number he had written down.

'I don't think I shall be needing help,' she said, and her soft young voice was low and edged with apology, for she did not want her words to sound like a snub.

'You never know. You're on your own there—except for Old Bill—and you might one day feel you need a friend. I shall be that friend.'

'Thank you,' she returned graciously. 'I shall remember that.'

They said good-bye outside the entrance to the Greenwood and Jody made her way to the lift. Turlough was nice, she thought, and it was kind of him to offer to be her friend in need. However, she could not envisage a situation in which she would call upon him for help.

It was after six before Conor got back to the hotel. Jody was curled up on the couch reading a book she had bought while on her travels through the city. Slowly she uncurled herself as he entered; he stood there staring down at her, a strange expression on his face.

'You move like a kitten,' he said, then frowned and moved away so abruptly that she actually felt hurt by the action.

'Did everything go off all right?' She stood up but remained by the couch. Why had he frowned after passing a remark that was plainly meant to flatter?

'All was most satisfactory.' His dark eyes flickered over her from head to foot. 'What have you been doing with yourself?'

'I looked at the shops in Grafton Street, then bought a suit and a dress. After that I had some lunch, then went into the park.' She avoided mentioning Turlough, and had no idea why.

'So you've had a good day?'

'Very good, but I missed you.' The admission came on impulse, and she coloured as she saw his eyebrows lift a fraction.

'You knew I'd be away all day.' His handsome face wore a slightly troubled expression as he looked into her eyes. He seemed to be reading what lay beyond their limpid depths, and she heard a sigh escape him that seemed like an indrawn breath of impatience.

'Yes, I know, Conor, but it would have been lovely to have been with you all the time.' She could not help it; she had to say what was in her mind.

'Jody,' said Conor sternly, but gently for all that, 'please remember that ours is a business partnership, nothing else.'

Her colour heightened rapidly as the blood rushed to her cheeks, for his meaning was patently clear.

'Of . . . of course I'll remember,' she stammered. 'I . . . I never regarded it as anything else.'

'Good.' He changed the subject, asking to be shown what she had bought. She went to her room and brought back the dress and suit.

'Do you like them?'

She watched his face anxiously and saw his dark eyes narrow as he said, 'It's not important that I should like them, Jody.' And then, noticing the crestfallen look on her face, he added, 'However, I like them very much. I must compliment you on your excellent taste.'

She said nothing, but took the garments away again. She felt a strange emptiness within her and was soon admitting that Conor's cool indifference was causing her pain. Yet what did she expect? *She* might be in love with *him*, but *he* was certainly not in love with *her*. She was his business partner, and also the 'child' he felt it his duty to care for. Jody bit her lip, wishing she were older so that he would not adopt this protective attitude towards her.

She wore the white cocktail dress for dinner and took a long time over her appearance, using a little colouring and lip rouge, brushing her hair till it shone. She took a last glance at her reflection in the mirror and liked what she saw.

Conor was waiting in the sitting room when she came from her bedroom; she studied his expression intently, her heart beating just a little too fast. His eyes flickered over her, taking in the slender waist, the delicate curves, immature but delectable for all that. His eyes came to rest on her face, and he seemed to be drinking in a picture which delighted and vexed him at one and the same time.

'You look very lovely.' He spoke as if he had to, flattering her in spite of himself. 'And what is that intriguing perfume?'

'Joy—it was terribly expensive!'

'But worth it. You must not forget you are rich now.'

'It's not easy to remember all the time.'

He was coming towards her; she quivered with expectancy, cheeks glowing, eyes bright with excitement. Desperately she yearned for physical contact, and it was as if her will was fleetingly ascending over his, for he took another step, bent his dark head, and kissed her full on the lips. Through the throbbing tumult of her emotions she was vitally conscious of the warm moisture, the hardness that thrilled, the mastery of the action, the arrogant assurance that she would not raise any protest. Perhaps, she thought as his hands took her waist possessively, there was a chance that he would fall in love with her. Why not? Obviously he found her attractive, for otherwise he would not be wanting to kiss her.

When his lips left hers, she waited, breathless, to see if his reaction would be the same as before. But no—there was a half-smile on his face as he said, 'Come, I don't know about you, but I'm more than ready for my dinner.'

They dined at a small table in a corner screened from the main expanse of the large restaurant by attractive potted plants and trailing ivies. There was a candle on the table set in a tall red chimney, and a tiny flower arrangement in a dainty ice-blue vase.

'This is nice!' Jody looked around at what she could see through the foliage of the plants. 'I like your hotel, Conor.'

'I'm free tomorrow,' Conor said, bypassing her comment. 'Is there anywhere you would like to go?'

Her eyes lit up at the idea of a full day's sightseeing with Conor, but she said she had no idea where she would like to go.

'I don't know anywhere yet,' she reminded him.

'Then we'll go to Powerscourt, which isn't too far at all from Dublin. We can then go for a drive through the countryside if you wish.'

'You're being very kind to me,' she quavered. 'Haven't you any business to do tomorrow?'

He shook his head, his attention now with the wine list that had just been handed to him. 'Nothing tomorrow, no. The following morning I have a meeting, and immediately after lunch we'll be on our way back to Rushwood.'

They set out at ten o'clock the following morning and drove at a leisurely pace to the old-world village of Enniskerry and shortly afterwards the Jaguar was bowling along an avenue of giant two-hundred-year-old beech trees which formed the impressive entrance to the stately home which, tragically, had been seriously damaged by fire a few years previously. But the elegant walls remained, rising above the impressive terraced gardens from where the Sugar Loaf, one of the summits of the spectacular Wicklow Mountains, could be seen against the sunlit Irish sky.

There were ornamental pools and long terraces, a lovely walled garden and a fountain spraying its sparkling waters sixty feet into the air. And not far from it stood the two winged horses of Fame and Victory. Jody several times exclaimed at the beauty of her surroundings, and she was ever conscious of her companion watching her, an expression of amused tolerance on his handsome face. It was the Japanese garden she liked the best, though, for there she could scramble over water-strewn rocks, cross delightful little bridges or sit in a pagoda-like building and shelter from the sun.

'Well, have you enjoyed the day?' Conor was inquiring when at last they were back at the hotel.

'It was wonderful! Thank you, Conor, for giving me such a happy time.' Sincerity looked out from her lovely eyes, and gratitude as well as she added, a huskiness edging her voice, 'I've never been so happy in my life—not since I was very small.'

They were in the sitting room, and for a long moment he stood looking down at her, an unfathomable expression on his aristocratic face.

'There's no need for such gratitude, Jody,' he assured her gently. 'It was a pleasure for me too. I thoroughly enjoyed the change . . . and the company.'

She shone up at him, and suddenly, without warning, there was a frown between his eyes and he seemed angry with himself. His voice had lost its gentleness when at length he spoke to tell her to go and change for dinner.

There was a letter waiting for Jody when she arrived home. It was from Rochelle, and a feeling of foreboding struck Jody as she picked it up from her desk where the maid had placed it.

Rochelle had written to say that as the new owners of her house wanted to move in, and as the flat was still not ready for occupation, she was planning a prolonged stay at Rushwood Castle. She had already made her booking and had it confirmed.

'So although you do not want me as a friend, I shall come as a guest. It would have been nice for me to have shared your suite, but I am sure I'll be given special accommodation, seeing that I am the sister of the co-owner of the hotel. . . .' There was a little more, but rising anger made further reading impossible for the moment. Sister! It hadn't been 'sister' a few weeks ago when Jody had begged Rochelle to let her stay in the flat for a while until she took her exams and then found herself a job! No, at that time Rochelle had derided Jody's claim to a relationship! At last Jody scanned the rest, then screwed up the letter and tossed it into the wastepaper basket. A few moments later she was knocking on the door of Conor's study.

'Come in.' He glanced up from some papers on his desk to look inquiringly at her. She stood a moment, thinking how handsome he was, how noble his features and aristocratic his manner and bearing. Sunlight shafting through the window brought out the silver at his temples, accentuated the noble, finely chiselled lines of his face. 'What is it, Jody?'

She came slowly into the room and stood by the desk. 'Rochelle wants to come here to stay for a while.'

'She does? That will be nice for you.'

'I don't want her,' stated Jody baldly. 'She and I don't get on. I . . . I feel inferior . . . uncomfortable . . .' Jody shook her head, frowning darkly. 'Please say she can't come.'

'This is a strange attitude for you to take, Jody.' Conor threw his pen on the desk and leant back in his chair. 'You and Rochelle seemed to get along quite well when she was here before.'

'We didn't. Rochelle and I have never been close. . . .' Her lip quivered as memory swept in and she saw herself as the odd one out, saw Rochelle basking in the praise and attention she was always receiving, not only from Philip but from his wife also. Jody had been nothing; she had felt her very presence in the house to have been a mistake on her adoptive parents' part, knowing without any doubt at all that if they'd had their time to live over again they would never have adopted her—or any other child, for that matter. Their lives were wrapped up in Rochelle; she was their pride and joy and they made no attempt to hide the fact—no, not even from Jody, whom they fed and clothed and tolerated, because in a weak moment they had been tempted to adopt a second child. They had given her a good home . . . but no love. Rochelle had known the position from the first, and sometimes Jody used to wonder if Rochelle's attitude towards her was the result of what she saw in her parents' treatment of her. Perhaps if they had given her love then Rochelle would have done so as well.

'I don't think you can refuse to have Rochelle here,' Conor was arguing logically.

'She says she's already booked in as a guest.'

'She has?' with a lifting of his eyebrows. 'In that case, there is nothing you can do. We haven't the right to refuse accommodation to a guest if we have that accommodation available.'

'Can't we say we're full?'

'It's obviously too late. You say she has already made her booking, so in that case it must have been confirmed.'

Jody bit her lip till it hurt. The issue seemed so important that she felt she must battle on to get her own way. 'I'm a partner,' she said gently, 'and so surely I have a say in who shall stay here and who shall not?'

'If you had known earlier what she intended, then I suppose we could have said we were booked up, but as it is, I'm afraid you'll have to get used to the idea of Rochelle coming over here. How long is she staying?' His eyes were curious; it was plain that he failed to understand just how upset Jody was by the letter.

'She mentions a prolonged stay.'

Conor merely shrugged his shoulders. 'I expect you will get over this aversion, Jody. After all, you and she have lived together for a number of years.'

She nodded dumbly and turned to the door. She heard Conor ask where she was going, and he now sounded a little anxious, she thought.

'I'm going over to see Old Bill. He should have finished work by now,' she added, glancing at her watch.

'There's no need to make yourself unhappy over this, Jody.' Conor's voice had sharpened; she could not tell whether concern or impatience was the cause.

Old Bill was in his neat little kitchen, standing by the stove, a fish slice in his hand. Jody saw him as she passed the window. His smile came swiftly when, after knocking, she lifted the latch and walked in.

'Hello,' he greeted her. 'How was Dublin?'

'Very nice.' She was not surprised to see his smile vanish. She knew what her voice sounded like.

'Trouble.' It was half-statement, half-question. 'Something wrong, little Jody?'

'Rochelle's coming here for a prolonged stay.'

He had been basting the contents of the frying pan, but now the implement was idle in his hand.

'A prolonged stay? But surely you have control over that? She can't stay any longer than you want her to.'

'Yes, she can,' returned Jody in a dull tone. 'She's booked in as a guest.'

There was a marked silence as the two looked at one another across the small kitchen.

'Have you spoken to Mr. Blake about it?' Old Bill inquired of her at last.

'Yes. He says I can't do anything about it. She's booked her accommodation and there's no way I can stop her coming here and staying as long as she likes.'

'Can she afford a long stay . . . ?' Old Bill stopped abruptly, nodding his head. He knew how much Rochelle had inherited from her parents. He also knew, as Jody did, how much Rochelle had sold the business for. Rochelle could live permanently at Rushwood Castle if she wished.

'You remember what she was like with Conor,

don't you?' Automatically, Jody moved towards the door separating the kitchen from the sitting room, and she stood there, eyes brooding and shadowed, reflecting the misery within.

'Yes, I do, fawning on him and making eyes! She's a bad one, that. Mr. Blake'll have to watch himself— but I daresay he's clever enough to see through anyone like Rochelle.'

'She's very beautiful.' With a backswitch of memory Jody was recalling Conor's cool indifference when she had talked to him about Rochelle. He had seemed totally to lack interest, and Jody remembered feeling relieved by his attitude. 'I could be worrying unnecessarily,' she added, speaking her thoughts aloud.

'You feel that if she should be fortunate enough to attract him, and become his wife, then your position would be uncomfortable?'

'Unbearable!' she exclaimed, so swiftly and emphatically that Old Bill's pale eyes widened with sudden perception. He opened his mouth to ask a question, then closed it again. There was a sad and anxious expression on his face as he turned back to his task of basting the piece of fish that was browning in the pan.

Jody walked into his cosy sitting room and stood by the window, her fingers absently touching the new drapes, tracing a curve round one of the large red peonies. Old Bill was most fortunate in his view, for at one end of his well-sheltered garden there was a gap where a dead tree had been taken out, so he had a magnificent vista of lough and mountains. Today the sun had been vanquished by cloud and over the mountains there could be seen towers of cumulus cloud, heavy with rain. The greyness lent a bleak and eerie aspect which suited Jody's mood,

Silhouette Desire

95p EACH

- ☐ 328584   **CORPORATE AFFAIR**
  Stephanie James

- ☐ 328592   **LOVE'S SILVER WEB**
  Nicole Monet

- ☐ 328606   **WISE FOLLY**
  Rita Clay

- ☐ 328614   **KISS AND TELL**
  Suzanne Carey

- ☐ 328622   **WHEN LAST WE LOVED**
  Judith Baker

- ☐ 328630   **A FRENCHMAN'S KISS**
  Kathryn Mallroy

All these books are available at your local bookshop or newsagent, or can be ordered direct from the publisher. Just tick the titles you want and fill in the form below.

Prices and availability subject to change without notice.

SILHOUETTE BOOKS, P.O. Box 11, Falmouth, Cornwall.

Please send cheque or postal order, and allow the following for postage and packing:

U.K. – 45p for one book, plus 20p for the second book, and 14p for each additional book ordered up to a £1.63 maximum.

B.F.P.O. and EIRE – 45p for the first book, plus 20p for the second book, and 14p per copy for the next 7 books, 8p per book thereafter.

OTHER OVERSEAS CUSTOMERS – 75p for the first book, plus 21p per copy for each additional book.

Name ....

Address ....

....

and a shuddering sigh escaped her. Why couldn't she do something about this new and unexpected situation? Why should she allow herself to be depressed like this? Anger mingled with resentment, while through it all rose her newfound confidence and her determination to become more mature so that she could assert herself. Rochelle would come to Rushwood, there was no doubt of that, but there was no reason why she should be allowed to remain indefinitely. Jody straightened her shoulders and lifted her head. Rochelle would *not* be allowed to remain indefinitely. She would leave when Jody told her to!

'Do you know what day Rochelle is coming?' Conor asked the question of Jody the next afternoon when they were in the Corrib Lounge ordering tea. Conor did not usually have tea, but Jody had managed to persuade him to keep her company, much to her surprise and gratification. As two sightseeing tours had been arranged for that day there were only a few guests in the lounge, so Conor and Jody were able to have a secluded table by the window where the view was over part of the castle grounds to the turretted gate and stone bridge spanning the river. Through another window could be seen the Corrib and three lush green islands poised like flakes of paradise itself on the silken waters of the lake. Beyond rose the Connemara landscape, fearsome and magnificent, its gun-metal-grey summits darkly outlined against downy white puffs of fair-weather cumulus clouds.

'I asked Esther. Rochelle will be here the day after tomorrow.' Jody's voice had lost its lightness, her eyes their glow. Esther was one of the receptionists; she also looked after the bookings and arranged all the sightseeing tours. 'Only two more days . . .'

Jody let her voice trail off because she felt that Conor had no patience with her attitude regarding Rochelle's visit to the castle.

'You've not changed your mind about letting her share your rooms?'

'No, I haven't changed my mind.' Jody looked resolutely out of the window in her quest for something to say that would let him see she wanted the subject dropped. 'I rather think it's cold out there on the lough today.' The hotel's white pleasure boat was being tossed a little, but that did not seem to bother the ardent anglers trailing their bait and hoping to make the record catch of the season.

'Lapping wavelets are necessary for good fishing.'

She nodded, conscious of his stare. 'I was walking on the lakeside when the breeze came up.'

'So I see!' Amusement in his voice and in his gaze. The breeze had whipped her hair into a spangle of tawny brown dappled with auburn glints. Automatically, she raised her hand in a futile attempt to put it back in order.

'I forgot to comb it when I came in,' she said, a hint of apology in her voice which brought an amused smile to Conor's lips.

'It looks very charming,' was his comment, and his smile deepened; she had not expected flattery, and it was revealed to him in her eyes.

The tea tray arrived. He watched her fill his cup and then her own. He handed her the cakes; she was conscious of his interest, the way his expression would change, and she wished she could read his thoughts. He was so charming with her; warmth flowed over her, then suddenly she felt a chill at the idea that he might not always be like this. She might one day do something to anger him, and then she would see a change, would be the subject of the arrogance which she knew was a permanent part of his makeup, a trait inherited from his noble ancestors, overlords of a bygone age.

He reintroduced the question of Rochelle, saying quietly, 'Am I to take it that you have no intention of keeping your sister company while she is here?'

'She isn't my sister.'

Conor's lips twitched, and she coloured, well aware that he was looking upon her attitude as childish.

'Sister or no—are you intending to leave her to her own devices all the time?'

'I have jobs to do, and I intend to continue doing them.'

'Jobs?' with a lift of his eyebrows. 'Such as?'

'The flowers.' Didn't he realise by now just how devoted she had become to the tender task of cutting and arranging flowers for all the main rooms of the hotel?

'Oh, yes, the flowers.' Conor picked up his teacup and put it to his lips. So casual, thought Jody, and bit her lip. 'I remember.'

'But don't notice?' His indifference hurt. She lowered her lashes so that he would not see.

'I do notice, my dear.' Gentle the tone, but Jody felt he was just being kind to her and that he had not noticed at all. She remembered at home, in the old days, when, on impulse, she had gathered wildflowers from a piece of waste ground and made a posy for the sideboard. Even if anyone did notice, comments were rare, praise even rarer. Mostly the comments came only when the flowers were dying and her mother would say, 'Will you throw those flowers out, Jody? They're beginning to make the water smell.'

'How is Bill these days?' Conor asked, breaking

the long, rather strained silence that had fallen between them.

'He didn't want the damp course—but I told you that, didn't I?'

Conor nodded his head. 'The work's started, though.'

'He still grumbles, but he knows it's for his own good.' Her warm, gentle voice carried a ring of affection.

Conor said, looking at her with an unfathomable expression, 'You think a lot about Bill, don't you?'

'He was my only friend when I was at home . . .' She stopped, not having intended saying anything like that.

Conor was frowning slightly, his glance curious. 'Surely, if you were adopted, then you must have been loved?'

She made no answer for a space, considering the question and wondering how to answer it. At last she said, feigning lightness which she supplemented with a smile, 'What I meant was, Bill was my only friend outside the home.'

Conor's gaze was steady and piercing. 'Have you any idea why your parents left everything to Rochelle and nothing to you?' he asked, and Jody shook her head.

'Not really. But Rochelle was clever and could help Father in his business. She has a brilliant mind and at only sixteen she was keeping the books. I did tell you that Philip was a builder, didn't I?'

'Yes. . . .' Conor became thoughtful. 'So Rochelle kept the books, and began when she was only sixteen. She must be highly experienced by now?'

'She is,' agreed Jody. 'She practically ran the business—well, the office side of it.'

Conor made no further comment, and as a couple

joined them, the matter was not again brought up. As he was leaving her, Conor said quietly, 'If you'll come to my suite about an hour before dinner, I'll go over the accounts with you. It was customary for Austin and me to have a small share-out every quarter, then the large one at the end of the year. Your share is due—'

'But I've had money from you,' she interrupted. 'More than I shall ever need!'

He smiled at that and shook his head. 'What you've had is nothing to what you now have to come. It was merely in the nature of an advance, so that your immediate needs could be met. It will be deducted from what is now due to you.'

She felt embarrassed by this talk of money but realised that she would have to get used to it. She asked what time he wanted her to go to his rooms and he said about seven o'clock.

'I'll change before I come, then,' she said, smiling.

It was inevitable that she should be thinking that after tormorrow evening she would not be having Conor all to herself at dinner. It was the one meal she delighted in, and at intervals during the day she would catch a glimpse of what the evening would bring: candles and flowers, sparkling crystal and heady wine. Excellent food, impeccable service . . . and the one person in the whole world she would choose as her companion, Conor . . . with that redoubtable attraction which had been too strong for her right from the start. Conor . . . with his courteous gallantry, his gentleness, his infinite understanding. But his amused tolerance, his almost fatherly manner at times, the occasional sternness when his voice would be sharp, his dark metallic eyes harder than ever. . . . Those were the things she disliked, resented, reminding her as they did of the gap in their ages, a gap which to her meant nothing but which to him seemed to be a barrier keeping him at a distance.

Often her mind would dwell on the possibility of his one day falling in love with her. It would be a miracle, wondrous and thrilling. And only to imagine it invariably set her pulses racing.

What should she wear? she was asking herself when, after showering, she stood before the mirror, wrapped in a towel, staring at her reflection.

She had brought a hand-printed silk evening dress —small flowers on a moss-green background. The style was simple, with a high neckline and short puff sleeves. She gave a small sigh on admitting that it did absolutely nothing to add to her age, yet on the other hand it was the prettiest dress she owned. She was dressing for Conor . . . all the time she dressed for him, hoping he would notice her and yet, conversely, she would not have him guess at her feelings, for that would be too embarrassing to endure.

His suite was rather more severe than hers, but all was in perfect taste just the same. In the sitting room there was a comfortable sofa to one side of a white marble fireplace, and two matching armchairs to the other side. A desk stood a little distance from the high wide window, and on two small occasional tables were matching Chelsea-Derby groups. The chandelier was Waterford crystal, as were the four matching wall lights. The dark blue carpet covered the entire floor; the drapes of midnight-blue velvet came right down to meet it. A man's room, with all those leather-bound books and the paintings of horses. On another wall were hung works by Monet and Degas, and Jody remembered Conor once telling her he favoured the impressionists.

Conor, immaculate and distinguished in an eve-

ning jacket and white frilled shirt, did not immediately invite her to sit down but looked her over for a
moment, his eyes unfathomable as they slid from her
face to her feet and back again.

'You look beautiful, Jody.' It was as if the words
were dragged from him against his will, as if he were
incapable of controlling his feelings. A smile fluttered to Jody's lips as she stood there, inside the
room but framed in the doorway like some exquisite
painting.

'I . . . I hope I'm not t–too early,' she stammered,
wishing her heart would not race so, or her pulse
quicken like this every time he looked at her in the
way he was looking at her now.

'Not at all. Come right in and sit down, my dear.'
My dear. . . . He often said it, but tonight it
sounded different in some unfathomable way, creating a tension within her, and an atmosphere profound and impalpable where she was conscious of a
bond being created between them that had nothing
to do with their business partnership.

Slowly she did his bidding; he came close as she
sat down, and the clean male smell of him assailed
her nostrils as he stood over her for a moment in
silence and friendliness. She twisted her head to
meet his eyes, but they became veiled on the instant
and she felt somehow that the moment was lost, that
if she had not been so anxious to note his expression,
something quite dramatic would have happened.

'Can I get you a drink?' His voice seemed tense,
not like him at all, and an unmistakable ring of
impatience came through to her, which she at-
tempted to ignore.

'I'll have a sherry, please, Conor.' Her voice was
calm, betraying nothing of the wild tumult within
her; she was here to talk business, and she meant to

show Conor that she could be mature, businesslike when necessary.

After giving her the drink, he poured one for himself, then sat down opposite her and talked for five minutes or so about various aspects of the business and the profits. There were a few renovations to be done, and Conor was asking her if she agreed to these. She had to quell the impulse to say she would leave it all to him, as she was sure that what he planned would be all right. But in her determination to appear more capable and mature, she questioned some of the expenses he talked about. He smiled faintly, and she began to wonder if he read her mind. However, he explained about the expenses which would be incurred, then, lastly, he told her what the renovations to the cottages were going to cost. She listened to it all with interest, while her thoughts sped fleetingly to Rochelle and the way she would conduct herself in a situation like this. Conor would instantly have evidence of Rochelle's business acumen . . . and he would probably admire her greatly because of it.

'And now for the financial aspect, as it benefits us both immediately.' Conor rose as he spoke, and moved over to the desk, beckoning Jody to follow him. He made her sit down while he explained what the reports were all about. And at last he put before her two cheques which she had to sign below his signature, which was already there.

'You will see that we are both to take the same amount at this stage. This usually never varies until the end of the year, when we have a more itemised report and take out most of the profits between us. You do fully understand? If you don't, then tell me, Jody, because it's important that you know what's going on.'

She lifted her face and smiled into his eyes. 'I've understood it all up to now,' she said.

'Good. Then you're ready to sign the two cheques?'

'Of course.' He was handing her a pen, but all she saw was the amount written on the cheques, and her eyes widened in disbelief. 'This . . . this isn't m-mine. . . .' She shook her head dazedly. 'It's a f-fortune!'

A low laugh escaped him. 'I rather thought you hadn't fully appreciated what you'd inherited, Jody. You're a very wealthy young lady.'

She continued to stare at the cheque which was made out to her.

'There is the possibility that business could be bad at times,' she heard Conor say, 'but that doesn't happen very often. Rushwood is famous throughout Europe for shooting, and Lough Corrib for fishing. Perhaps you haven't yet fully grasped that the main emphasis here at Rushwood is on sport of many kinds.'

'I have—but I suppose it hasn't registered properly.' Yet she knew about the fishing and that Rushwood would be crowded in the autumn when the shooting season began. Then, there was the golf, of course, and tennis and horseback riding.

'Well,' said Conor with an amused smile as he watched her hold the pen she had now taken from him, 'are you going to sign?'

She nodded and signed, then put the pen on the desk. Conor picked up one of the cheques and handed it to her.

'What on earth shall I do with it?' asked Jody shakily, thinking of all those years during which she had had practically nothing to spend. It had not been pleasant, watching Rochelle with her expensive clothes and cosmetics, or knowing she was taking a holiday abroad. She had earned it, Jody was told when on one occasion she had protested that it wasn't fair that Rochelle had so much and she had nothing.

And now . . . she was wealthy. . . .

'You must learn to spend, my child,' Conor was saying into her thoughts. 'Save some, by all means, if you want. I'll give you advice on investments, if you like.'

He took up the other papers and dropped them in a drawer. Then he moved away, and she followed, the cheque held as if it were hot.

'Conor . . . ?'

'Yes?'

'I really don't know what to do with it.' She felt overwhelmed, unable to assimilate the important position she held and which in these past few minutes her partner had, with patience and understanding, tried to put over to her. 'If . . . if you would keep it for me . . . ?'

He was shaking his head, so she broke off, feeling helpless, regretting this loss of the newfound self-confidence which she had assumed had come to stay.

'You'll soon get used to the idea of having money,' he said gently, then shook his head on noting her bewildered expression. 'Come here, child. . . .' The grip of his hand brought her close, and pleasure brought a smile to his lips.

She curled her fingers round his hand, her senses powerfully and disturbingly affected by the gentleness with which he drew her quivering body to him in a strong, protective embrace.

'What a child you are,' he murmured close to her cheek. 'And yet . . .' His voice trailed away; Jody lifted her head to look intently at him. She saw a muscle move in his throat, out of control, saw the narrowed aspect of his gaze, the slow tightening of his mouth. Instinctively, she guessed at the struggle taking place within him, knew that as her self-appointed protector he felt he ought not to kiss her . . . even while he wanted to. . . .

She quivered against him, enticing in the one and only way that came to her—the primitive tempting put down originally to Eve. Her hands touched his neck; her soft yielding body pressed close, melding its contours with the muscular hardness of his. She felt the increased pressure of his arms about her, knew he was conscious of her soft breasts flattened against his chest. She raised her head, tilting it back, her eyes wide and limpid, as inviting as her softly parted lips.

'Jody . . .' His voice was hoarse, his breathing ragged, and in his dark metallic eyes was reflected a sort of primordial passion that at once thrilled and frightened her. What had she done . . . ? No time to answer as he said, 'You have asked for it!' He was losing control, carried away by the sweetness of her body, the delight of her lips, the deliberate tempta-tion of her hand as it slid within his shirt after a button was undone.

With a sort of dazed wonderment, Jody was exploring, sensually experimenting as, with tactile pleasure, she flattened her hands against the sinewed tautness of his chest, then closed her fingers gently, tugging against the wiry dark hairs within their grasp. She felt him quiver as if his body had weak-ened fleetingly, caught in a spasm of erotic pleasure which robbed him of the power to think of anything beyond the moment and the tantalising creature he held within his arms. For Jody, the interlude was sheer ecstasy, the rapture of first love in all its pristine purity, the intimate, initial sensations filling her with wonderment and desire, depriving her of clear thought, driving her to fight for more . . . and to conquer. She heard a soft and ragged whisper at her throat, knew the bliss of his tender passion as his long lean fingers closed gently round one high firm breast. She was poised in breathless expectation of some movement, her tingling nerves balanced on the edge of rapture as she waited for that ecstatic moment when his fingers would move to caress the nipple. A spasm shook her as his fingers closed, pinching gently, persuasively, and in the heated frenzy of the moment she could not hold back the words that came straight from her heart.

'Conor . . . I love you. . . .' Had she spoken them aloud? She felt Conor stiffen against her, and for one agonising second she was convinced he would draw away from her. Why, oh why, had she let her heart's secret escape!

'It's time we were going down to dinner.' The words were slowly and softly spoken, with infinite kindness and concern. His eyes were darker than she had ever seen them; it was as if pain and regret were shading them.

He knew she loved him, and because he could not reciprocate, he pitied her—oh, so deeply he pitied her! Tears filled her eyes, then spiked her lashes before falling down onto her cheeks. If only she could put the clock back a moment . . .

'Conor, I—'

'There's no need for tears, Jody.' With tender emotion he looked into her eyes; she knew he was thinking of her great-uncle and asking his forgiveness for this lapse, this action which, born of a weak moment, had brought anguish to the girl he had meant to protect. 'Let me dry your eyes.' His handkerchief was already out, his hand beneath her chin. She looked at him, blinking as the handkerchief came near. And then she closed her eyes, a sob reaching up from the very heart of her. This was pain and misery the like of which she had never known, nor even visualised. She wished she were dead—or back with her parents and Rochelle, for the pain then was a mere pinprick in comparison to this.

Chapter Seven

There was a look of determination in Jody's eyes as she faced Rochelle across the breakfast table. Conor had not put in an appearance for the past three mornings, and so the two girls had breakfasted together. Rochelle had been at the castle for just less than a week and the previous day had taken it upon herself to order Old Bill about, having come upon him sitting quietly on a small stone bench, taking a rest and enjoying the sunshine and the scenery. Rochelle had asked him in tones of familiar arrogance what he was supposed to be doing.

'I'm clipping the edges of that lawn over there,' he had answered, deliberately omitting the respect he had previously been obliged to extend to her.

'In that case,' Rochelle had said, 'go and do what you are being paid for.'

When Jody had gone over to Old Bill's cottage,

the incident was related to her, with the instant reaction on her part being a flood of anger so strong that it threatened to choke her. However, Rochelle was not to be found, and so Jody had to wait until the morning before being able to tackle her.

'As I've said, Rochelle, you are merely a guest here. You have no authority to give orders to our employees, so please refrain from doing so again.'

'He was wasting his time!' stated Rochelle, eyes glinting. 'I used to watch him, all the time, knowing just how lazy he could be! He didn't get away with it when he worked for us, so why should he get away with it now?'

'It so happens,' returned Jody with dignity, 'that Paddy is the head gardener here. It's very likely he's going to resent your interference. Paddy gives the orders, not you—or even I, for that matter. And I'm sure that even Conor would not interfere; he'd respect the authority of the man he's employed as overseer.' Jody reached for some toast, her cheeks tinted a little, but otherwise there was no sign of her being flustered or unsure of herself. From the first she had decided to stand up to Rochelle, and had been moderately successful. True, there were times when Rochelle, in her arrogance and forcefulness, had overridden Jody, but those occasions were few and far between. As for Rochelle's relationship with Conor—well, up till now Jody had no complaints. Conor was fully occupied with his work during the day, and in the evenings at dinner he had been polite to Rochelle, and that was all. Undoubtedly Rochelle was furious at her lack of success, but that did not deter her from trying. She persistently used all her charms; she flattered Conor's methods, congratulated him on some alterations he had made during the past year. Her smiles were winning, her glances coy. She used her lovely hands; she knew exactly how to move her head so that her glorious hair would be brought to the notice of all who happened to be near.

'She makes me sick!' Jody had exclaimed to herself more than once.

'I shall talk to Conor about Old Bill,' decided Rochelle at length. 'I can't imagine how he came to be persuaded to employ the man at all! He had his day a long time ago and is ready for an institution.'

'He'll never go into an institution!' snapped Jody, eyes blazing at the derogatory way Rochelle was speaking of her friend. 'I shall see to that! When he's too old to work and to look after his cottage and himself, I shall find him accommodation in the castle.'

Rochelle laughed at her, a jeering derisive laugh that set Jody's temper even more on edge.

'You always were too soft with that old tramp! It often used to make me wonder what your own background was.'

Colour crept slowly into Jody's cheeks. This was an insult directed at her dead father, and the fury rising within her was more than mental. It formed a tight ball in her stomach which seemed slowly to rise to her throat.

'I am asking you to leave,' she said tautly. 'We have nothing in common, Rochelle, and added to that, I have no intention of being jeered at and insulted in my own home. I feel sure your flat will be ready quite soon; meanwhile, you can live in an hotel near to it.'

'I shall leave just when it suits me,' broke in Rochelle harshly, 'and not before. I'm a guest here, and your asking me to leave is a slight which I am not willing to take lying down. I shall speak to Conor immediately after we've finished breakfast.'

It was just about half an hour later that Conor sent for Jody; she was in the lobby chatting with two American couples who had just arrived by taxi from Shannon Airport. They had been thrilled with the pictures of the castle, they said, but were even more thrilled with the real thing.

'I only hope you will have good weather,' Jody was saying when one of the porters came up to tell her that Mr. Blake wished to speak with her in his study.

Her heart was beating a little too fast as she made her way through the lobby and several large public rooms to the corridor off which Conor's study was situated. Scarcely had she knocked than she was invited to enter, which she did, head aloft because she meant to hold her own.

'Sit down, Jody.' Conor indicated a chair, which she took. 'What's all this about your telling Rochelle to leave here?'

'She insulted me.' It never occurred to Jody that she might look and sound peevish, or that Conor would consider her to be irritatingly childish. But he did, regarding her with frowning impatience as he said, 'I rather think you're far too ready to take exception to anything Rochelle might say. How did she insult you?' His voice was hard but curious, as if he were ready to listen in spite of the conclusions he had already drawn.

'She hinted that I'd come from a disreputable background.' Jody somehow couldn't meet his steady, piercing gaze, and as she lowered her eyes, she heard his indrawn breath of asperity.

'Feminine bickering! I refuse to be brought into it!'

She did raise her eyes then, a militant sparkle in their depths. 'You were the one who sent for me! I didn't ask you to be brought into it!'

'Jody,' he said authoritatively, 'that will do. You're being thoroughly childish. Now, just put all this nonsense out of your head and try to be friends with Rochelle.'

'You wouldn't listen to me, but you listened to Rochelle!' Tears were close, choking her voice because of this dissension which had come between them owing to Rochelle's animosity. 'I want her to leave here!'

Conor drew a breath, tossed his pen on the desk and leant against the back of his chair. 'Just what is the matter with you?' he demanded. 'If Rochelle is such a thorn in your side, then keep out of her way.'

'It's impossible to keep out of her way all the time; she makes sure of that.' Should she tell Conor about the way Rochelle had treated Old Bill? A moment of deliberation was enough to make her abandon the idea. Conor would only treat it as childishness, as he did everything else. 'Forget what I've said.' She turned abruptly, anger and pain fighting for supremacy. She felt lost and alone and her feet dragged as she made for the door. But then she turned again, her face tense, a sort of quiet desperation about her as she came slowly back into the centre of the room. Conor stood up, seeming to move automatically to the other side of his desk.

'Please, Conor,' she begged, 'don't be like this with me—I can't bear it if we're not friends. If you would only try to understand how I feel . . .' Before she could even think, much less control the impulse, she had flung herself into his arms and was weeping softly on his breast.

'Jody . . . my child, you mustn't cry.' So gentle the tone, but beneath it lay that impatience, that tinge of regret and anger against himself. 'What have I done . . . ?' He broke off after speaking almost inaudibly. She caught the words, though, and knew just what he meant.

Sadly, she disengaged herself from arms that had come clear around her, and she moved away, again feeling lost and alone . . . and fleetingly her thoughts went to Turlough, who had promised to be her friend.

The pale lavender eyes were narrowed and troubled as they looked into Jody's pallid face. 'I can't believe it!' he almost shouted at last in his anger. 'What is Mr. Blake thinking about to take her on as his secretary!'

For a moment Jody could not speak for the misery within her. It filled her whole being, choked and stifled her. It was as if some terrible disaster had overtaken her, vanquishing her cherished hope that one day she would win her partner's love.

'It wasn't as if he didn't know that I hated having her here,' she managed at last, even now quite unable to understand why Conor should have employed the girl whom she, Jody, disliked so much.

'I expect she pushed herself at him!' No comment from Jody, and Old Bill went on furiously, 'Always did have an eye to the main chance, that one!'

'Conor had been saying he must get a secretary; it was the perfect opening, and she seized it. I had already told him how efficient she was,' added Jody with a shuddering sigh of regret.

'Is she to stay indefinitely, then? What about this flat she says she's bought?'

'I don't know. She hasn't confided in me, but I wouldn't be surprised if she decided to find a tenant for it.'

'So she *is* staying indefinitely?'

'It seems like it. Conor has said she can keep the room she is occupying at present.' Words still came with difficulty because she was so utterly cast down by what she had just learned from the malicious, triumphant lips of Rochelle.

Jody, determined on having her own way, had approached her again, less than twenty-four hours after telling her to leave, and said forcefully, 'I insist on your leaving, Rochelle. You've gone out of your way to sneer at me, to make yourself objectionable, to deride Old Bill and harass him, and I won't have it. No matter what Conor says, I'm having my own way in this. I'm telling you to pack your bags and leave!'

"You are?' with a twist of those crimson lips. 'Well, little Miss Arrogance, it might interest you to know that at nine o'clock tomorrow I take up the post of secretary to your partner!'

Stricken by the news, Jody had been almost unable to breathe. It was as if a hand of ice had clutched at her heart. She had also been unable to tell herself that Rochelle had lied, simply because a lie could not benefit Rochelle anything. 'You know,' Rochelle had continued with an amused sneer, 'you're so absurdly transparent. You want Conor for yourself, but to him you're just a child, and a fractious one at that. The only reason you don't want me here is that you're afraid, isn't it?'

'Of . . . of what?' quavered Jody, white to the lips.

'You know of what—oh, don't deny it, girl! You

give yourself away all the time. He must be heartily
sick of the stupid, infantile advances you make!'

Unable to stand any more, and with sheer undi-
luted misery swamping both her anger and her self-
confidence, Jody had left Rochelle and with leaden
steps had made her way through the deep park to
Old Bill's little cottage. It was a haven, just as the
prefab used to be, and she walked in at his invitation
and sank into the winged armchair. With her story
unfolded, she had wept a little, and then her mind
seemed to be constantly focusing on the open,
friendly face of Turlough O'Neill. . . .

'I suppose,' murmured Old Bill, breaking into
Jody's reverie, 'Rochelle's hoping Mr. Blake will fall
for her.'

'I expect that's her aim. She told me—when she
was here before—that he was interested in her.'

'And was he?'

'He didn't seem to be, but now . . .'

'Perhaps it's only convenience on his part, Jody,
love,' said Old Bill soothingly after a moment of
pondering. 'He needed a secretary—you yourself
mentioned it a week or so ago. And we have to
admit that Rochelle's efficient; she'll save him a
tremendous amount of work. Yes, I'll bet it's only
for convenience that he's taken her on.'

'If she's with him, taking letters, working with
him, he's bound to . . . to . . .' Jody could not continue; she buried her face in the chair and wept as if
her heart would break. 'I . . . I couldn't bear it if
he . . . he married her!'

'I once said he was the kind of man who'd see
through her, Jody, and I still believe that. She's a
coldhearted cat, and I can't see Mr. Blake being
deluded into thinking she's a nice girl.'

'I don't want to go back,' she was saying sometime later as dusk dropped down on the mountains and the lake and the mellowed castle walls.

'Then don't, love. Stay and share my meal. It's not much, but the vegetables are fresh and the pudding's nice too—out of a tin, but tasty and nourishing.'

She managed a smile, recalling the way he used to tell her about his housekeeping. 'Shall I help you to prepare it?' she asked, and because he knew it would help to occupy her mind for a while, he accepted eagerly, asking her to peel the potatoes.

It was dark when at last she left the cottage. She had tried not to think of Rochelle dining with Conor, sitting at the table which she, Jody, had shared with him so many times. That was all over now, though; there would be no more happy, intimate dinners with just the two of them, chatting and laughing, enjoying each other's company.

Old Bill walked part of the way with her, but once through the inky blackness of the deer park, she said she would be all right on her own.

'The hotel lights are all on,' she said, her eyes going to one of the windows of the lounge where coffee was always served after dinner. Conor and Rochelle would be in there, talking quietly. . . .

But she was mistaken, as it happened, for Conor was just coming from the direction of the keep when she reached the forecourt. She saw him quicken his steps, noticed the frown on his forehead, and wondered if it was caused by anger or anxiety.

'Where the devil have you been?' he demanded, reaching her and towering above her in the most frightening way. 'I've been looking everywhere. Why didn't you come in for dinner?' He looked her over; she had the impression that nothing would have given him greater satisfaction than to box her ears!

'I had a meal with Bill,' Jody said, and lifted her head, injecting a note of militance into her voice. 'I don't *have* to dine in the hotel, do I?'

'Don't adopt that attitude with me, Jody,' he warned. 'If you must have your dinner with Bill, then at least let me know.'

She shrugged her shoulders, marvelling at her temerity as she said defiantly, 'I'm not answerable to you for my actions, Conor, so please don't *you* adopt that attitude with *me!*'

'Be very careful,' he rasped. 'I'm responsible for you, and therefore—'

'In no way are you responsible for me, and I resent your attitude! You seem to have taken upon yourself the role of guardian—well, I don't need a guardian, so there!' She had no idea just how childish the last two words sounded, but Conor was so angry that he found nothing amusing in them at this time. Her absence had troubled him; he had not even finished his dinner, but had excused himself, leaving Rochelle fuming in the knowledge that he was far more concerned about Jody than about etiquette or good manners.

'You'd better come up to my room and we'll talk,' he said curtly, and before she could dodge out of his way, he had her by the arm and was propelling her towards the high, wide entrance to the hotel lobby. 'No nonsense,' he warned close to her ear. 'I'm in no mood to provide a nine days' wonder for the staff!'

'I shan't make a scene,' she retorted stiffly. 'And there's no need to grip my arm so tightly; I shall not run away!'

He turned his head swiftly, and she caught the

compression of his lips, and the sound issuing from them that was like the hiss of a snake.

'It would seem you are rapidly coming out of your shell,' he gritted. 'But don't try me too far, Jody, or you might get your bottom smacked!'

'Oh . . . you . . . !' Hot blood rushed to her cheeks and she twisted against his hold. It was a futile effort, and as they were entering the lobby, she refrained from any further attempt to free herself.

Once in his sitting room, she moved to the window, turning her back on him even while every fibre within her cried out for his arms, his warm lips, the rapture of his caress.

'You have obviously taken exception to my employing Rochelle as my secretary,' was Conor's perceptive observation as soon as he had closed the door.

'It has nothing to do with me.'

'Do you mind turning round? I'm not used to addressing people's backs.'

It was a moment before she obeyed his request, and when she did, she just stared at him in silence, her lips quivering uncontrollably, the shadows in her eyes lending a haunting beauty to her face. She wondered if he was aware of the tumult within her heart, the deluge of pain and sadness. . . . He must be, seeing that he knew she loved him.

'I needed a secretary, Jody.' Conor's voice was gentler than she would have expected. 'Rochelle's obviously extremely efficient. She was wanting a job, and so it suited us both that she should come and work for me.'

'But it didn't suit me—and you didn't care.' Jody had not meant to utter words like those, especially after she had just said that what he did had nothing to do with her.

'There's no need for you to come into contact with her too much.' Conor still retained that quality of gentleness, and his voice with its soft inflection was more hurtful than its harshness of a moment before. She looked at him across the room, knowing that he pitied her because of the way she felt about him, and bitter resentment welled up inside her. She did not want his pity! She would show him she did not need it, either. She would ring Turlough, who had promised to be her friend in need.

However, she thought better of it, afraid she might start something she would come to regret. But events were shortly to bring another change of mind, for at dinner one evening, not only had Rochelle taken the place usually occupied by Jody, which was the one opposite Conor, but she received almost all of Conor's attention, being consulted about the wine, advised on the most appetising dishes, and in the conversation that took place while the meal was being eaten, it was a plainly marked fact that Jody was the odd one out, simply because the two were discussing various aspects of Rochelle's duties. To Jody it seemed that Rochelle was all the time aware of her power and appeal, and it also seemed that Conor's behaviour was deliberate, that he wanted Jody to realise he was more interested in Rochelle than in her. And as time passed, Jody became so uncomfortable that instead of staying for coffee in the lounge, she excused herself and went to bed. The following evening she phoned Turlough and was fortunate enough to find him at home.

'So you decided to get in touch! I'd begun to think you wouldn't. What can I do for you, Jody?'

She was lost for words, not having rehearsed what she would say to him. 'I . . . er . . . just thought I'd ring and have a little talk. . . .'

'Something the matter?' he wanted to know, the question coming without a second's pause.

'Not . . . not really.'

'Would you care to come out with me this evening? We could go for a run in my car and find a little place to eat.'

'I'd like that.' Jody marvelled at the swift release of the weight on her spirits. 'What time shall I meet you?'

'In half an hour?'

'That'll be fine.'

'I'll call for you.'

Silence. Jody could not make up her mind. What would Conor say if he saw her getting into Turlough's car? What had it to do with him anyway?

'Yes, that will be all right, Turlough. I'll be waiting for you at the entrance.'

'Great! I'll be with you in thirty minutes, then!'

Jody held the receiver for a moment or two, staring at it unseeingly. What had she done? And how far did she intend to go? She replaced the receiver and slowly went from the sitting room to the bedroom. Let the future take care of itself, she decided, and it was with more enthusiasm than she would have expected that she carefully chose what she would wear for this first date with Turlough.

He was waiting when she came from the lobby; she got into the car and they were driving away in less than thirty seconds. The pearl-blue sky of evening lay over the mountains and the lake as they bowled along the magnificent drive, and then there was darkness as the trees closed around them. But once through the high wrought-iron gate, the landscape was aglow again with twilight hues, while the clear outline of a full moon promised a flood of silver when eventually darkness fell.

'Want to talk?' invited Turlough as the car wound its way along a leafy lane between ochre-coloured walls on both sides of which were the grounds of the castle, a wonderland of beauty with their massive trees and shady woodland paths, all created by a previous owner of the castle and estate, a titled Irish gentleman who, with his wife, spent a lifetime beautifying the immense grounds, to say nothing of the castle itself.

'I'm happy just driving,' answered Jody noncommittally.

Turlough slanted her a glance, then returned his attention to the road. 'Something's wrong. I promised to be your friend, Jody, and I meant it.' His voice was low and so very attractive, with that Irish lilt and soft pronunciation. 'Confide if you want; I'll respect any confidences you'd like to make.'

She said after a small hesitation, 'It's Rochelle— my adoptive sister. I mentioned her when I was talking to you about my parents.'

'I remember. I gained the impression that you and she didn't have very much in common.' Turlough pulled far to the left, almost touching the wall in order to make room for another car to pass. 'What about Rochelle?'

'She came to Rushwood to stay for a while, supposedly until her flat was ready—I think I told you about her buying a flat?'

'Yes, that's right. So she's come to visit you—and you're not too happy about it, apparently?'

'As you've already guessed, we don't get on together.'

'If you don't want her, then surely you can tell her it's not convenient for her to stay.'

'I did tell her I don't want her, but . . . but Conor . . . Mr. Blake's now employing her as his secretary.' The catch in her voice could not possibly escape him and, as he just happened to be close to a part of the road that had been widened to make passing easier, Turlough pulled over and stopped the car.

'So she's to live at Rushwood permanently?' He was frowning, and Jody tried to remember just how much she had told him about Rochelle and her character.

'Yes, it seems like it.' Jody related the scene when she had asked Rochelle to leave. 'She then dropped the bombshell; Mr. Blake had engaged her as his secretary.'

'What's she like?' inquired Turlough curiously.

'Very beautiful. At home she could have any man she wanted, but she said . . .' Jody stopped abruptly but, noticing Turlough's look of inquiry, she decided to continue. 'Rochelle always said she wanted to marry a handsome man with position and wealth.'

Turlough pulled his lip. 'Mr. Blake'll fit, all right.'

'That's what I think.'

'You're not in love with him yourself, are you?'

The question, coming out of the blue like that, caught Jody off-balance, and she coloured as she heard a low whistle escape Turlough's lips. 'You are?' Half-statement, half-question; for a moment he seemed a little flat, but then, to her relief, he gave a slight shrug of resignation. 'I must say I'm not surprised, for I hear that Mr. Blake's an exceptionally attractive man.'

Jody changed the subject, telling him about Rochelle's attitude towards Old Bill, relating the incident when Rochelle had told him to get on with his work.

'She sounds like the real catty type,' said Turlough with a frown. 'What was the old boy's reaction?'

'He didn't take much notice, but he told me about it, and I tackled Rochelle. She adopted an arrogant manner and said Old Bill was ready for an institution.' Jody could not have explained why she was saying all this to Turlough, but it did seem they had known one another for a long time.

'Will she have any influence with Mr. Blake? I mean, could she cause Old Bill to get the sack?'

'Not while I own half of Rushwood!' Determination gave force to her words. 'Old Bill is really happy and comfortable for the first time in his life, and I shall fight to keep it that way—if I have to, that is!'

'Good for you! But you're pretty young and, if you'll forgive me, not too sure of yourself yet. I really meant it, Jody, when I said you might need help.' Turning his head, he looked into her eyes; she saw the sincerity in his, heard it in his voice, too, mingling with anxiety as he added, 'Let me take you out at least once a week, Jody. It will be something for us both to look forward to, and it'll also give you an opportunity of talking. If Rochelle makes herself too high and mighty, we shall think of something to bring her down to earth again. But don't hesitate to phone me if, at any time, you feel you can't cope.' He paused a moment, his fingers twisting the ignition key. 'Are you going to make a permanent date? We'll have a meal together at least once a week?'

'Yes, I'd like that, Turlough.'

He shifted the car into gear and moved away from the hedge. 'I hope you'll like the cosy little eating house I'm taking you to,' he said, smiling in the dimness of the car, which was purring smoothly along the road, headlights flaring, picking out the eerie outlines of the trees. 'It's a couple of miles beyond Cong, in a delightful spot overlooking Lough Mask. The café's called Clonbur House.'

'I'm sure I shall like it,' returned Jody eagerly.

'Feeling better now we've had that little talk?'

'Much. Thank you, Turlough, for being patient and understanding.'

'A pleasure,' he returned, laughing lightly. He patted her knee in a friendly, reassuring gesture. 'Remember what I've said. Just you pick up that phone and get in touch if ever things get on top of you.'

She nodded, feeling grateful that she was not entirely alone. She had a good friend in Turlough, and even though she could not visualise his ever being able to help her in any constructive way, at least he was there, a sympathetic listener to whom she could pour out her troubles if they became too much for her to bear alone.

Clonbur House was small and cosy, as Turlough had said. An original Irish farmhouse with a thatched roof of yellowish brown straw, it had been renovated and slightly enlarged for its conversion to a café. But it still retained many of the farmhouse's attractive features, such as the main hearth, open and at floor level. Always these hearths occupied the long axis of the farm kitchen, Turlough told her. Never were they against a side wall or in a corner. The walls were stoutly constructed of stone or clay. Pseudo-antique tables of fine quality lent atmosphere, while amber lights and the glow from the peat fire lent colour. The soft crimson glow was reflected on the hearth and on an assortment of cast-iron pans of the kind used by the farmers' wives for making the meals and baking the delicious whole-meal soda bread.

'Well?' Turlough smiled at Jody across the table, and she smiled back.

'It's lovely!' she exclaimed. 'So intimate and warm!'

'And so different from the restaurant at Rush-wood Castle?'

'Indeed, yes. You could fit this charming little place in one corner.'

The food was excellent, Jody having frest trout caught a few hours previously in Lough Mask, while Turlough chose salmon, also caught that day in the lake. For dessert there was a mouth-watering choice from a pastry trolley, then coffee afterwards.

'Keep me in the picture, won't you?' Turlough was saying as he drove her back to the castle two hours later. 'I want to help, Jody, for as I said, you're very young, and you're all alone as well.'

'I have Old Bill,' she murmured, but with a small sigh. 'I don't suppose he could be of much help, though. . . .' Her voice trailed off, for she was not intending to reveal her thoughts, which were on the possibility of Conor's falling for Rochelle and decid-ing to marry her.

'Which reminds me, I mentioned him to my uncle, and he said he'd very much like to meet Old Bill.'

'I'll have a word with him, then.'

'I could either bring Uncle Shamus here or call for Old Bill and take him along to the caravan.'

'All right. I'll tell you what he prefers. He might not want to bother, though,' she felt obliged to add. 'He's fired up with enthusiasm at present, eager to get his little cottage all shining and shipshape.'

No more was said for the time being and, in any case, they were already passing the gate lodge, Jody receiving a salute of respect from the lodge-keeper, who had come out to open the gate for them when he saw the lights of the car. The bridge over the river was reached and passed; then Turlough pulled up right in front of the main entrance to the hotel.

Jody turned to him with a smile. 'Thank you so much for a lovely evening, Turlough. I shall look forward to the next one.'

'And when will that be? We haven't said which evening we're going to meet.'

'Would Thursday be all right for you?' she asked after a small pause. She had thought that Saturday would be a good choice, but hesitated about suggesting it, feeling that Turlough would probably want to do other things on the weekend.

'That'll be okay with me,' he returned quickly. 'If I don't hear from you before, I shall be here promptly at half-past seven next Thursday evening.'

She agreed, and would have slid from the car, but before she could do so, Turlough's arm encircled her gently and she felt his lips on her temple. She had no idea by what impulse she turned, offering him her lips. She had never meant to, much less to slide her arms about his neck. And it was only when she was alone in her bedroom, by the open window, watching the moon-splashed water of the lake ripple in the eddy of a night breeze coming down from the mountains, that she was able to pick out an answer from the jumble of her mind. Her behaviour out there had resulted from the need for comfort, the desire for reassurance that she was not quite alone in what she had to face. Turlough would be there—good, kind Turlough of the soft voice and kindly eyes. Somewhere, thought Jody with a smile, there was a lucky Irish colleen all unsuspecting of the happiness and good fortune that would one day come her way.

Chapter Eight

Pale gold darts of sunglow cut through the delicate foliage of the birch trees to create diamonds on the dew-spangled webs in the hedgerow. To the other side of the narrow path was the Cong River, moving lazily beneath the early-morning sun, where a family of swans glided gracefully along towards the cut-stone bridge over which Jody had just come. She stood alone in the shadows, watching the cygnets, remembering how small they were a few short weeks ago—just fluffy balls and now almost as big as the swans, but very different because their plumage was a dull brown and still rather fluffy in comparison to the sleek whiteness of their parents. All was motionless but for the flowing river and the swans; not even a bird or a butterfly, not a rabbit in the undergrowth. Jody moved on, feeling she had the whole wide world to herself, and as she looked around her at the grandeur, she thought it must have been like this before man came on the earth to ravage its pristine beauty. Ireland, though, had so much beauty still undefiled, because Ireland was fortunate enough not to have such things as vast reserves of coal, that black invidious substance which, in England, had been so important in helping man in his greed to ruin vast regions of what once had been country equally as beautiful as this, in its own unique way, of course. Here were the wild mountains of Connemara, the vast unpolluted Lough Corrib with its numerous lush green islands, many of which held secrets of past history or were steeped in folklore. On some lived the little people, the fairies and the leprechauns, and some were sanctuaries for birds and other wildlife.

She wandered on slowly, and in the deep silence, time seemed to hang suspended, and she stopped again, enveloped in the wonder of it all.

And then she saw him, the perfectly cut trousers and snow-white shirt enhancing his lean good looks. His hair shone in the sunlight; Jody could almost see the fine iron-bright threads at his temples. His stride was long and confident, like that of an athlete at the very peak of his career. Jody felt her heart lurch, and a pulse began to throb in her temple. The palms of her hands felt damp. Why should she feel like this? Perhaps it was because she and he had not been alone together for any appreciable time since Rochelle had arrived at the castle, this time to stay indefinitely.

He stopped a yard or so away from her, then came forward unhurriedly. 'You're up and about early,' he observed, the dark metallic eyes sweeping her from head to foot. She was wearing slacks and a light blue turtleneck sweater, which, having shrunk in the wash, fitted her tender young curves rather more snugly than when she had first bought it.

'So are you,' she returned, feeling gauche and yet conscious of an attempt to appear cool and confident. Until Rochelle came, she had been acquiring poise and self-confidence; she had begun to give polite orders to employees, and had been able to converse with the guests in an easy, fluid way that had even amazed herself at times. But now she felt inadequate, because of the way Conor had treated her lately, with a sort of patient indifference. He seemed loath to be unkind, yet he gave her the impression that he wanted to keep her at a distance.

'Do you often walk at this time of the morning?' His face was inscrutable; Jody could not tell whether he was talking for the sake of it or not.

'Sometimes I do, yes.' She shifted on her feet, vaguely aware that her white tennis shoes had let the damp penetrate through the canvas. 'It's so quiet; you have it all to yourself.' She lifted her face, and he could not help but notice the sadness marring the limpid beauty of her eyes. She saw his expression change in some subtle way, and then her gaze was drawn fascinatedly to the pulsating nerve at the side of his throat. What kind of emotion was responsible for that uncontrol? she wondered. Once he had been so easy to read and understand, because he had nothing to hide, but now—and she told herself doggedly that it was only since the arrival of Rochelle—he was an enigma to her, his manner always guarded, sometimes to the point of coldness.

'You like the loneliness of the early-morning scene, then?'

She nodded at once. 'Very much. Oh, I like the life at the castle,' she added swiftly, in case he should misinterpret her admission, 'but it's pleasant to be on your own, to be close to nature as you are here, by the river, with the swans gliding along and the shadows of the mountains with their ever-changing colour as the sun rises higher and sheds its rays into the hollows.' She stopped rather abruptly, the colour fluctuating in her cheeks. 'I was intending to walk to the abbey. . . .' Her silence asked the question; her eyes begged for the answer she so desperately wanted.

'I'll walk that far with you, Jody.' His eyes travelled over her slender figure, rested on the cascade of brown hair for a moment before settling on her face.

'That'll be nice, Conor.' Subdued the tone, for she did not want him to regret what she knew was an impulse and change his mind, saying he must get back, as he had work to do.

They went at a leisurely pace along the bank in companionable silence, with the flax-yellow sun to the east, and eventually came to what was once the crowning glory of Cong, the Royal Abbey built by the onetime High King of Ireland, the powerful Turlach Mor O'Connor.

'It's so beautiful, even though its glory is all in the past.' Jody's voice was low and reverent, her eyes dreamy as she and Conor wandered about, picking their way among ancient gravestones clothed with bright green moss. 'I expect that for every gravestone we can pick out there are a dozen hidden beneath all this vegetation.' Jody had stopped, and she looked into the face of the man beside her, wondering if he would speak.

'You're a very sensitive child, Jody,' he said gently, and her heart gave a little lurch.

She looked away, then down at the smudged charcoal grey of the stone at her feet. Vaguely, she was aware of trying to read words that were indecipherable. The years and the elements had taken their toll of the craftsman's painstaking work of long ago.

'Sh-shall we walk over there?' she asked awkwardly.

'As you wish.' He was close, his hand touching hers, deliberately. A smile quivered to her lips, for it was a tender moment, and one of impulse as things turned out, because Conor's fingers enclosed her small hand in his. 'You'll need assistance in climbing over these humps and ploughing through the vegetation,' he murmured.

Jody said nothing; silently she savoured the intimacy of the situation, for they were quite alone among the noble ivy-clad ruins of the abbey, built over eight hundred years ago on the site of an even more ancient building, the Monastery of St. Feichin.

Slowly they made their way through the ruins, stopping now and then to look at something of particular interest, and Conor with his knowledge would offer information for which Jody was avidly receptive.

'It's hard for visitors to believe that this small village of Cong was once of such great importance, that this abbey was one of the most important seats of learning in the world.'

'In the world?' repeated Jody, thinking he must have meant just Ireland.

'Yes, the world, Jody. You must remember that the Augustinian monks ranked high where arts and letters were concerned, and this abbey used to house over three thousand students at a time. Ireland was a land of culture, showing an example to many other countries of the world.' The vibrancy of national pride came through the familiar softness of his voice, and Jody looked up into his face, feeling proud of her own Irish blood. Conor smiled into her silence and tugged at her hand. 'Let's wander through here and take the path between the trees. The walk to the little bridge is a favourite one of mine.'

'Yes, I love it too,' she said eagerly. 'I came with Rochelle, but she . . .' Jody stopped abruptly, not because of giving away Rochelle's grumbles that her new shoes were being ruined by the wet grass, but because the intrusion even of the name seemed out of place here, where Jody was so happy, having Conor all to herself.

'Well?' he prompted, slanting her a curious glance. 'What about Rochelle?'

She met his gaze and wondered why she should have this strong impression that he was keenly interested in what her reply would be.

'Nothing,' she returned. 'I don't want to talk about Rochelle.'

'You still don't get on with her?'

'We see each other only at mealtimes, and not always then.'

'She mentioned, among other things, that you seem deliberately to avoid her.'

'Then she's right.' Jody's voice quivered because she was remembering her onetime ardent wish that she and Rochelle would be close, just like real sisters, so that they would each have someone of their own whom they could love and trust. 'I don't want to talk about her,' she said again, and would have withdrawn her hand but, as if anticipating the action, Conor tightened his hold. She lifted her face, unaware of the brightness in her eyes. A sigh escaped her companion but there was no sign of the impatience Jody had noticed on several previous occasions.

134

'It's a pity you can't bring yourself to forget your grievance,' he said.

Something in his intonation made Jody say swiftly, the hint of protest in her voice, 'I don't hold it against her for what our parents did, if that is what you're suggesting, Conor.'

'I wasn't suggesting anything like that. I have no idea why you two girls, who have lived together for years as sisters, should now have become almost like strangers.' He paused a moment; she felt his fingers moving over hers in a sort of abstract way as his brow creased in thought. 'It isn't Rochelle's doing, Jody—and I have to stress this. She's said several times that she wants to be close to you, really close, but you shun every advance she makes, and she was saying she feels so hurt and snubbed that she can't make any further approaches.'

It was natural that as he was speaking Jody's temper was rising. What a hypocrite Rochelle was! And a liar, too! All Jody's dislike welled up and increased, but she made no comment, knowing too well from previous experience what Conor's reaction would be. It had been the same at home, with Rochelle always being able to put on an act of sincerity. Jody recalled how, in the very beginning, Rochelle had fooled their parents with her outward show of affection for the little girl whom they had adopted. Protective and kind was the veneer, while underneath was the true Rochelle, and this had very quickly been revealed to the receptive mind of a six-year-old child. It could not have been otherwise. And now Rochelle was at it again with her hollow hypocrisy and the mendacious way in which she was approaching Conor, who, Jody now strongly suspected, had himself broached the subject of the lack of warmth existing between the two girls.

'Isn't this a beautiful walk—this one that goes over the bridge?'

Conor's eyes narrowed as he slanted her a glance. 'You say you don't want to talk about Rochelle, but it would be better if you did, Jody. I want you to be friends.'

'It isn't important,' she returned casually.

'But it is, Jody, very important.'

'Why?' The brief question escaped swiftly, born of the sudden idea that had come into her mind. 'Why is it very important, Conor?' The sentence was jerky, spoken on a catching breath. 'Do . . . do y-you think a lot about . . . about Rochelle?'

There was a fleeting silence, but during it Jody felt her chest go tight with the agony of suspense. And then all feeling left her as she heard Conor say, 'Yes, Jody, I do think a lot about Rochelle.'

Old Bill hadn't left the cottage when Jody arrived there, and naturally he was surprised by a visit so early in the morning. Jody, thinking she would never know how she managed to finish her stroll with Conor, had come straight here, to Old Bill's little cottage, as soon as Conor had left her in the lobby of the castle. She could not possibly have gone in to breakfast, whether Conor was there or not; she had no appetite, not with her stomach muscles knotting up as they were doing.

'What's up, little Jody?' Old Bill looked intently into her face. 'Rochelle again?'

'She's managed it.' Jody's voice was dull as she went past the old man into the sitting room. 'Conor's just told me that it's important for Rochelle and me to be friends because . . . because h-he's in l-love with her.'

'In love?' Old Bill shook his head vigorously. 'I

don't believe it! Did he actually say a thing like that?'

'Not in so many words,' Jody had to own, then went on to add, 'But when I asked him if he thought a lot about her, he said yes, he did think a lot about her. . . . No, Bill, there was no mistake; he definitely said it, and meant it.'

'I still don't believe it!'

'Because you don't want to, Bill.'

'Surely he has more sense than to fall for that one!'

'Rochelle's very beautiful and very clever; you know that from past experience.'

'I'd not have thought she'd be clever enough to hoodwink a man like Mr. Blake, though.'

'Beautiful women are often quite irresistible to men. It's nothing new.' Jody sat down in the wing chair and stared unseeingly through the window. She could just see the highest turretted walls of the castle, ochre-gold in the sunshine. 'If he marries her, I'll have to leave, Bill, for I couldn't bear to stay.' Tears of pain filled her eyes, but she held them back; the look of quiet concern on the old man's face told her that he was suffering already, and the last thing she desired was for his suffering to be increased, which it would be if she were to burst into tears.

'If you leave, then I shall leave, too,' he said after a long moment of considering. 'I'd never have her giving me orders again.'

She would give him only one order, thought Jody, and that would be to pack up and leave this little cottage, the first real home he had ever owned. A lump rose in Jody's throat, preventing speech, and after a while she stood up and said she was going, but that she would come over that evening.

'Stay for a meal, then,' he suggested, 'and we can

talk about this business, as I still can't accept that Mr. Blake would every marry Rochelle.'

But as the days passed, it did seem to Jody that Conor was falling in love with Rochelle. She would see them walking together in the grounds, sometimes appearing to be making some sort of a survey, and Jody would be reminded of Rochelle's efficiency when running Philip's business. At other times Rochelle and Conor would appear to be strolling together for mere pleasure. Always Jody was crucified by the conviction that Rochelle was about to get what she wanted.

'And to think, if it hadn't been for me, she and Conor would never have met.' The words were spoken to Turlough while Jody and he were having dinner at Clonbur House the following Thursday. 'It's ironic, isn't it?'

He nodded but remained silent, his manner one of deep concentration. When at last he did speak, it was to remind her of something he had said to her on a previous occasion. 'If you remember, Jody, I said that if Rochelle became too high and mighty, then we'd find something to bring her back to earth?'

'Yes.' She nodded. 'I remember.'

'Well, why don't I pretend to be your fiancé? Neither she nor Mr. Blake is going to like that idea, are they?'

'You . . . my fiancé?' Jody put down her knife and fork and stared at him in bewilderment. 'I don't understand, Turlough. What good would that do?'

'Well, at least it would produce some results, and if I'm not mistaken, it would shake up Mr. Blake and make him reconsider.'

'He isn't exactly engaged to Rochelle yet.'

'But you seem to be convinced he soon will be.'

'Yes, I do agree, but—'

'If you're to act at all, then it must b. proposes to her, because Mr. Blake, 'efore he honourable man he is, wouldn't go back on'g the once it was given. Now . . .' Turlough atord reached for the salt, but then just held it in his h., 'I can imagine a situation where Mr. Blake's going stop and consider the consequences of your marrying me. I'm going to move in; I shall be the husband of his partner. I shall have some say in the running of the business—'

'Turlough, this is wasted conjecture. I wouldn't do a thing like that to Conor—give him such anxiety.'

'You're resigned to him marrying Rochelle and your having to leave the castle? You've stated quite firmly that you'll leave, and that Old Bill will have to leave as well.'

She moistened her lips. Turlough's idea had come too suddenly, rendering her unable to think clearly, to visualise the situation which would arise if she should decide to fall in with his suggestion that they pretend to be engaged.

'Let's not talk about it,' she begged. 'I was enjoying our meal . . .' Her voice trailed to silence as she saw the sceptical lift of his eyebrows.

'You're not enjoying it at all, Jody, dear. However, we'll not talk about it just now. When you go home tonight, just sit quietly and consider my suggestion. Believe me, Jody, it would pull both those people up with a jerk.'

Jody nodded in agreement, for although a clear picture was still absent from her mind, she could imagine some consternation for both Conor and Rochelle if she were to announce her engagement to Turlough. Of course, Conor would be exceedingly puzzled by her action, simply because he knew with-

was he whom she loved. Well, seeing as out doubt made any decision yet, Jody saw no she ha dwelling on something which in the end pro prove irrelevant.

When the meal was over, Turlough drove her back to the castle, but as it was only a quarter to ten, they walked across the beautifully manicured gardens towards the wooded region behind which was the lake. It was a lovely summer evening with the sickle of a young moon bright and clear-cut above the equally sharp outline of the mountains. The lake rippled gently, driven by a warm languorous breeze blowing from the south.

Jody stopped to glance up. The castle in its hauntingly beautiful setting rose majestically above velvet lawns and terraces, the light flaring from its turrets throwing into relief the perfect proportion of its lines.

'Isn't it lovely?' Jody made a comprehensive gesture as she swung around again. 'I felt so thrilled at owning half of all this. How can I leave it, Turlough?' Jody's voice broke in the middle, and the next moment she was seeking comfort in his arms.

'Hush,' he murmured kindly. 'Don't cry, dear Jody. There's no question of your having to leave it. It's still yours, and no one can tell you to go.'

'But if Conor marries Rochelle . . .'

'That's something we're going to try to prevent—' Turlough's voice stopped suddenly, and he was pushing her away. Uncomprehending, she looked up into his face, and then her eyes moved.

'Conor . . .' He was there, with Rochelle, his face like thunder.

'What the devil do you think you're doing?' he demanded of Turlough. 'I thought Jody was with . . .' He stopped and turned his full attention on her, noticing her flushed face, the dampness on her cheeks. 'I took it for granted that you were with Bill.'

'I dined out with Turlough—Conor, this is Turlough O'Neill. Turlough, Mr. Blake.' The men looked at one another, Conor glowering and Turlough just waiting to see what Jody would do. She looked at the svelte, willowy figure of Rochelle and thought her dress to be as sexy as that of a model she had seen in a glossy magazine. She said quietly, 'Rochelle, meet my fiancé, Turlough O'Neill.'

'What did you say?' Conor's voice jerked, vibrant with anger and disbelief. 'Your . . . fiancé!'

'That's right, Mr. Blake,' interjected Turlough, taking his cue. 'Jody and I met some time ago in Dublin and have been keeping company ever since. I . . . er . . . hope we shall all become very good friends.' So glib, thought Jody, staggered by what she had done. An idea had become a reality almost without her being aware of it! She had been driven by an incomprehensible impulse, and the only explanation which eventually did offer itself was that she'd had an impulsive desire to hit back at both Rochelle and Conor—although why Conor, she could not understand, since he had every right to be keeping company with Rochelle if that was what he wanted.

Conor moved from Rochelle's side to Jody's, his metallic eyes boring into hers as for a long moment there was silence between and all around them. Jody's heart was beating overrate, but on the surface there was a sort of composure about her which surprised them all.

'Is this true, Jody?' Conor's voice was soft when at last he spoke, and Jody frowned as the idea of an undercurrent of pain reached her senses. Pain? Well, perhaps, because she had been seeing Turlough

without informing him of the fact. Conor still regarded himself as her guardian, and as such he
ought to have been kept in touch with what Jody
was doing. Yes, that was the reason for the pain—if
pain there was, of course, and Jody could not be
absolutely sure.

'Yes, Conor, it's true. Turlough and I are engaged
to be married.' What was to come next? she wondered. The step she had taken seemed to have put
her beyond control of her own future actions.

'I see'—grittingly and with an icy glint in his eyes.
'And when are we to expect a wedding?'

'Let me congratulate you, Jody, darling,' purred
Rochelle into the silence that followed Conor's
question. 'How nice to know you're settled, and with
such a charming young man. But you ought to have
told us, shouldn't she, Conor?' Dovelike eyes looked
up, and lashes fluttered as Rochelle glided close to
Conor and slipped her arm through his.

'I shall talk to you about this later, Jody,' he said
darkly. 'Come to my rooms at half-past nine in the
morning.' Not only had he ignored Rochelle, but he
had actually disengaged his arm. Looking at her,
Jody saw her mouth tighten to an ugly line in a face
that had lost much of its colour. How well Jody
recognised those signs of Rochelle's gathering temper! But she would not give Conor a demonstration.
No, she was smiling even now, because his glance
happened to light on her as he looked around in his
anger.

'I wondered,' said Turlough, as if the idea had just
come to him, 'if we could all go in and have a
celebration drink?'

Jody actually heard Conor's teeth grit together.
'Another time,' he snapped. 'It's late. Jody, I don't

want you out here at this time. You'll oblige me by coming indoors!'

'Mr. Blake,' said Turlough quietly, 'I resent your attitude. *I* shall see Jody safely back to the castle, after we have finished our stroll.'

Conor looked at him challengingly. 'Mr. O'Neill, *I* happen to be responsible for Jody, who is under-age—'

'I am not,' she interrupted, feeling she had to support Turlough while at the same time desperately unhappy at adopting this attitude with Conor. 'I'm eighteen and therefore entitled to do what I please. Turlough and I were having a pleasant stroll—'

"You weren't strolling when we came upon you,' intervened Rochelle with a silky laugh. 'You were . . . er . . .'

'Jody, I must ask you to come inside!' imperiously from Conor, and this time he gripped her arm so hurtfully that she had the greatest difficulty in smothering the cry which leapt to her lips.

She looked at Turlough in a way that caused him to nod and say resignedly, 'You had better go, Jody, dear. I'll give you a ring in the morning. Good night; sleep well.' He glanced fleetingly from Conor to Rochelle, said another good night, then strode away towards the place where he had parked his car.

Chapter Nine

Old Bill taken ill! It was Tommy who brought the news to Jody when she was arranging flowers in the dining room. He had come to the desk asking to see her urgently and had been sent into the dining room by Esther. Jody's face lost colour as the news was imparted to her from the grave-faced gardener.

'He came over early this morning to say he wasn't feeling too well and asked me to make his excuses to Paddy. I said I would bring you over, but he wouldn't have it. You know what he is, Miss Hendrick, very stubborn, and he became really worked up and angry when Lisa said you ought to be told. Then about half-past eight she went over with some porridge and he didn't seem too bad but when she went over an hour later he had collapsed and was on the floor. She came for me and we got him onto the couch.' He stopped and Jody saw him swallow convulsively. Old Bill had endeared himself to many people in the short time he had been at Rushwood Castle.

'I'll come over at once.' All Jody's own troubles subsided under this disturbing news. 'Has anyone rung the doctor?'

'We haven't a phone,' began Tommy, when Jody interrupted to say she would get to a doctor right away.

'It's his heart?' she asked, feeling sure it must be this.

'Well . . . I expect so, but he's always seemed so strong, in every way.'

It transpired that it was a heart attack Old Bill had had, and Jody stayed with him until half-past eight that evening, when, to her surprise, Conor came to the door of the cottage, knocked lightly and walked in. Tommy and Lisa had helped Jody to bring the single bed into the living room, where there was a fire and which was much more pleasant than the bedroom anyway, which had not yet been decorated.

'How is he?' Conor's voice was edged with concern as he came towards the bed. Old Bill was sleeping under the drugs given him by the doctor, and his breathing seemed to be normal.

'I want to stay all night, Conor.' Jody's voice was low but firm; nevertheless, Conor was shaking his head.

'I shall see that someone stays with him, Jody, but you must come back. You can't do anything here, and you need your rest if you're to come back tomorrow.'

Which was sensible, but Jody, tears gathering in her eyes, wanted only to stay with Old Bill all the time, for she feared he was going to die and she wanted to be with him at the end.

'Please let me stay.' All the fight was going out of

her already, and she realised that Conor could often make her feel like this these days. For his whole manner was one of mastery, his voice mainly carrying an imperious inflection whenever he spoke to her.

For herself, she had become distant after the morning five days ago when he had told her she was a fool to marry Turlough, and when she had argued, he had said with almost cruel frankness, 'You don't love him! You can't, can you, when you love me?'

She had coloured and turned away, saying chokingly, 'I shouldn't have said it—and you shouldn't have remembered.'

'Give this man up,' he had ordered, but Jody had doggedly tried to convince Conor that she had fallen out of love with him since meeting Turlough. In the end he had been forced to accept the engagement and from then on a coolness had existed which Rochelle had not failed to notice. As for Jody, she had become withdrawn from both of them, just as in the old days, when she was the odd one out, the misfit in a household of brains and efficiency and bold activity. Rochelle had been the star, just as she was now, for even the office staff at the desk sang her praises and said they didn't know how Mr. Blake had ever managed without her.

'I'm not letting you stay, Jody.' Conor's voice broke her reverie and she looked up at him from her seat beside the bed. 'I'm going over now to phone for a nurse to come in, but meanwhile Lisa might be persuaded to come over so that you can join me for dinner.'

'I don't want to join you for dinner.' She never did these days, and she was surprised that he should make the suggestion now.

'It so happens that I should otherwise be dining alone, as Rochelle's gone to bed with a cold.'

'She has?' Catty to feel glad, but Jody was certainly glad! 'In that case, I'll dine with you, Conor.'

He looked at her hard and long, opened his mouth to say something, then closed it again. Jody had the sure conviction that he had been about to ask her again to give up Turlough.

The nurse agreed to come, but it would be about ten o'clock before she was free. Lisa willingly offered to fill in until she arrived, so Conor took Jody away with him and together they walked in total silence through the deer park into the hotel gardens proper.

The meal was a disappointing affair, with neither Jody nor Conor speaking very much at all. And when it was over, she shook her head when he asked if she would take coffee with him in the lounge.

'I'm going to bed,' she told him. 'I want to be up very early tomorrow and go over to see Old Bill.'

'You're not going to see how Rochelle is?'

'No. If she's in bed, she won't want me disturbing her.'

'You're such a child, Jody, and so very transparent.' They had been about to leave the table, but neither had yet moved. Jody looked at him through eyes darkened with sadness and anxiety, for she was so sure that Old Bill had come to the end of his life.

'I'm not a child,' she said in husky tones. 'I wish you wouldn't keep saying it!'

'Your attitude towards Rochelle is childish, Jody, and if you are fair, you'll not deny it.'

'I resent her coming here. She knew I didn't want her . . .' Jody stopped, then added reflectively, 'You don't know everything, Conor, and so you haven' any notion what has caused this attitude of mine towards Rochelle. If you did, then perhaps you'd understand a little better.'

'Why not tell me, then?' Although he had asked the question, his tone was not encouraging, and Jody shook her head, rising from the table at the same time.

'It's not important that you should know everything,' was all she said, and with a final 'Good night,' she walked away, scalding tears filling her eyes as she wove her way through the lounge towards the lift.

Once in her room, she found herself with the sudden and unexpected urge to go and see Rochelle after all. Why, she could not have explained; it wasn't anxiety, since Rochelle only had a cold anyway.

Her quiet knock on the bedroom door was responded to immediately, and Jody could not help wondering if Rochelle was hoping her visitor would be Conor.

Rochelle was sitting up in bed, her diaphanous nightgown so low-cut that Jody was too embarrassed to look lower than Rochelle's face.

'So you dined in the restaurant tonight.' Rochelle's diamond-hard eyes swept over the charming ankle-length dress of coral nylon jersey which, owing to its texture, enhanced the youthful lines of her figure in a way that Jody herself was unaware of but had not escaped the notice either of Conor or of Rochelle.

'I dined with Conor, yes.'

'Because I wasn't there.' Rochelle reached for a tissue from the box and blew her nose.

'I'm not happy being the odd one out, Rochelle. For many years I was in that position—'

'Imagination!' interrupted Rochelle shortly. 'The trouble with you, Jody, is that you're always filled with self-pity!'

'I came to see how you are,' murmured Jody, and saw Rochelle's eyes narrow at Jody's deliberate bypassing of her comment.

'Do you really care?'

Jody shrugged her shoulders. 'I'd better go,' she said, moving towards the door.

'How is that old tramp today? How long is he expected to last?'

Jody froze; then the coiled spring of her tension shot loose. 'You're hateful!' she cried, eyes flashing venom at the girl she had so recently hoped would be her friend, the sister she had so desperately wished for. 'I detest you, Rochelle! Pity is totally alien to your nature, and if Conor marries you, he'll regret it within a month!'

'So it's all coming into the open at last. You're jealous, aren't you, Jody?' The jeering voice held laughter and contempt, and automatically Jody put her hands to her ears. 'Conor's mine, not yours, and just you accept that! Do you hear!' Jody, pale to the lips, said nothing, but took another step towards the door. 'You'll have to leave here once I'm married to Conor,' Rochelle went on. 'I hope you understand that? I have no intention of having you interfering in the running of this hotel, so you can begin thinking about selling out to Conor!'

At that Jody turned back to face the girl on the bed. 'I have no intention of leaving,' she told Rochelle, marvelling at the steadiness of her voice. 'Turlough will . . . will be my husband, and as such he'll have some considerable say in the running of Rushwood.'

'He . . . !' Rochelle stared, wrathful colour mounting her cheeks. 'Do you believe that Conor will have him, a stranger, interfering?'

'Turlough will not be a stranger; he'll be my husband, with a position similar to your own if you marry Conor.' On that parting shot Jody left the room and found her steps directed to the lounge, where just a few minutes ago she had left Conor. Yes, he was still there, his aristocratic, charming manner achingly evident to Jody as she watched him in conversation with two guests who she knew came from California. They had stayed at the castle on two previous occasions and were staying this time for no less than a month.

Jody halted by the bar, where an immaculately clad waiter was making coffee to be served fresh to the guests, along with liqueurs and crispy mint chocolates. Conor appeared to be totally relaxed on the comfortable sofa, his lithe frame clad in a Saville Row evening suit and a Jermyn Street shirt. He looked superb, a distinguished and compelling example of manhood combined with the suave confidence of the experienced hotelier. Inevitably, Jody's mind went to Rochelle, who, with her poise and self-confidence, her supreme ability with figures and flair for business, would undoubtedly be an asset to Conor if he should decide to marry her. But what of the other side of her nature—the side that had nothing to do with hardheaded profit calculations or schemes for improvements? Surely Conor wanted love in his life. Perhaps he believed Rochelle could give him love, though. Perhaps Old Bill was sadly mistaken in his prediction that Conor was far too shrewd to be deceived by the kind of facade Rochelle, in her cleverness, could assume.

As he had seen her and was getting to his feet,
Jody went forward, and said she would like to speak
to him when he had time.

'Is it important, Jody?'

'I think so, yes.'

He had finished his coffee, and so he excused
himself with a slight bow and a smile. A few
moments later, he and Jody were in his study.

'Sit down,' he invited, bringing forward a chair.
'You look troubled. What is it?'

She did not care for his standing over her; she
made a small gesture, and he sat down, faintly
amused.

Without preamble she said what she had rehearsed since coming from Rochelle's bedroom. She
watched anger grow in Conor's eyes, and bit her lip
till it hurt, but she continued until, at the end, his
eyes were smouldering with wrath. Never had she
seen him as angry as this, but she seemed to have
grown up suddenly and knew she must fight to hold
her own. She became profoundly aware of her
position as equal partner to Conor; she had as much
say in the running of the hotel as he. She knew that
Rochelle was her enemy and would utterly crush her
if she could, since already she had suggested that
Jody should begin to think of selling out to Conor.

'I mean it, Conor,' she said, and although it was a
deliberate lie, she had no compunction as she added,
'Turlough will have authority from me; he will share
with you the running of this hotel. His word will
carry equal weight with yours.'

Conor stared at her, and she thought it was
consternation more than anger which now looked
out from his eyes. This aspect he had not considered
any more than Rochelle had considered it. Had

Conor, too, taken it for granted that she would sell out to him in the eventuality of his marrying Rochelle?

'You're serious?' His expression had changed again; it was thunderous now, and she saw that he was keeping his anger on a tight rein only with the greatest of difficulty. 'You'd have this man Turlough sharing my duties here?'

'If we marry, then he'll want some work to do—'

'*If* you marry?'

'I should have said *when* we marry.' There was an uneasy edge to her voice which she hoped he had not noticed. She was thinking of these steps she was taking, each leading her deeper into an unreal situation, simply because she had no intention of marrying Turlough.

Conor's voice was harsh when presently he spoke. 'I shall not brook any interference whatsoever in the running of this hotel. If you marry, then your husband will have to work somewhere else.' His dark eyes smouldered and his mouth was tight. His whole attitude was one of ruthless domination which, she knew, was meant to disarm her.

But she managed to retain her courage, injecting a militant quality into her voice. 'As I am an equal partner, I have an equal say in what shall be done. It is my wish for my husband to share all responsibilities with you, and he must be consulted about all decisions which you might want to make.' She looked at him with a rebellious expression in her eyes. 'I'm not being pushed around, Conor, and the sooner you realise that, the better it will be for all of us!' And with that she rose from the chair in preparation to leave the room.

'Just what's happened to make you adopt this attitude?' Conor's voice was quieter, more familiar . . . and attractive to her ears. She swallowed convulsively, the lump in her throat making speech difficult.

'You must have known that when I married, things would have to change.'

'You haven't answered my question.'

'Nothing's happened—'

'It must have,' he said imperiously. 'And it's happened since dinner. Have you spoken to Turlough?'

'On the phone?' Jody shook her head. 'No, I haven't.' She paused a moment, but Conor seemed lost in thought and did not speak. Jody said quietly, 'Good night, Conor,' and made her departure from the room.

Old Bill was neither better nor worse when Jody arrived in the cottage at half-past seven the following morning.

'He's had a fairly comfortable night,' the nurse said as she gathered her things together in preparation for leaving. 'I've washed him but he hasn't had his breakfast. He said he wasn't hungry.'

'Hello, there, little Jody,' he greeted her. 'You're early. Couldn't you sleep?'

'I did sleep, yes, but I had every intention of coming early to see you. How do you feel?' She looked affectionately at him, thinking that at least he was comfortable, clean and warm, something made possible only because he had the cottage.

'I couldn't abide that sour-faced nurse,' he was saying after the woman had left. 'Is she coming again tonight?'

'Not if you don't want her to.'

'Tommy and Lisa seem to think I need someone with me in the night, but I don't.'

'Oh, yes, you do. Mr. Blake was here last evening and he sent for the nurse. You can't lie here on your own, Bill, and so we must find another nurse, one you'll like.'

But when the doctor arrived, he immediately suggested he make arrangements for Old Bill to go to hospital.

'Good idea,' agreed the old man, but knowing him as well as she did, Jody was quick to guess that he was trying to make things easy for everyone.

'I'd much rather have him moved to the castle,' she said quietly but in firm, decisive tones which would have surprised her adoptive parents if they could have heard. 'We have plenty of room, and it will be better all round, because I will be at hand the whole time.'

'Little Jody,' began Old Bill with an affectionate smile, 'it's good of you, love, but . . . well, let me go into hospital—'

'I can't *make* you come to the castle,' she interrupted, 'but I shall be hurt if you refuse.'

'It'll be such a bother. . . .' His voice trailed off and he closed his eyes as if he were already exhausted.

'It's no bother,' murmured Jody softly. 'It would be far more bother if everyone had to travel to the hospital to see you, wouldn't it?'

'I suppose so. . . .' His voice faded and his mouth seemed bluer than it had before.

Jody's heart gave a little lurch and she turned swiftly to the doctor.

'Is he very ill?' Her lips formed the words and the doctor nodded his head gravely. 'Then the castle is it,' she whispered. 'He is not going to die in a hospital!'

Conor agreed with Jody, affording her intense pleasure by his decision. Old Bill would be given a room on the first floor, one with a view of the lough and the mountains.

"You're very kind . . .' There was a catch in Jody's voice and her throat felt blocked. 'You have no idea what it means to me, Conor. Bill and I have been friends for a very long time.'

Conor looked at her with a softened expression. 'You're very sweet,' he began gently, then stopped as Rochelle came into the lounge where they were sitting. 'You're feeling better, obviously?' he said, smiling.

'Yes, much better, thank you, Conor. I'm ready to start work again.'

'You might as well take the rest of the day off. There isn't anything urgent at the moment.'

'Thank you.' Rochelle sat down without being invited, and crossed her elegant legs to show a shapely thigh against the split in her skirt. 'How is the old man this morning?' Her eyes were directed at Conor, but it was Jody who answered.

'About the same.' She believed he was worse but had no intention of telling Rochelle. 'He's coming to stay at the castle until he's fit again.'

'The castle!' Rochelle frowned her disagreement. 'He's going to stay here, in the hotel?'

'And why not?' Never before had Jody portrayed arrogance, but her voice certainly carried it now, and in no mean degree. 'It was either that or hospital, as he can't be left in the cottage.'

'I should have thought the hospital's the place for that old tramp.'

'Tramp?' Conor spoke at last, turning his eyes on her after having been only mildly interested in what the two girls were saying to one another. 'Is that how you regard him, Rochelle?' Soft the tone, but in stead of the attractive Irish burr, there was a hardness which appeared to startle the girl responsible for it.

Rochelle flashed him a smile and said purringly, 'I suppose you don't care to think of him as that, and I ought not to either, seeing that he now works at the castle . . . or did work here until this happened. However, I do suggest, Conor, that you retire him now, because he's far too old. I've seen him sitting down, resting, many a time, and thought how fatigued he was. Employees who don't work are a drain on any business, and when I worked for Father I sacked anyone who wasn't an asset to us.'

'Old Bill never gets tired,' snapped Jody, uncaring what Conor thought of her attitude towards Rochelle. 'He's marvellous for his age . . . and he's good for another ten years at least!'

'Hear, hear,' applauded Conor, much to Rochelle's discomfiture. 'He's an old soldier, and you know what they say about them.'

They never die. . . . But Old Bill was seriously ill, and it seemed very possible that he would not recover. Jody gave a deep sigh and blinked rapidly to hold back the tears. 'I must go and see Tommy,' she said, rising. 'He and Lisa have offered to help me move him.'

'I'll bring him over in my car,' interrupted Conor gently. 'Tommy's car is rather small for a job like that.'

Rochelle shot him a glance; he was not looking at her, so he missed the swift tightening of her mouth.

'This is absurd nonsense!' Rochelle was saying later when, after Old Bill was comfortably installed in his room at the castle, she and Jody happened to be alone for a few moments. 'Have you thought of the disturbance to the guests when he dies? And what about all the trouble it's going to cause Conor? If I had any say, I'd have him in hospital where he ought to be!'

'But you don't happen to have any say,' returned Jody, quivering on the edge of fury. 'I am the one who decides where Old Bill shall go.'

'You've managed to get Conor's approval of your stupid idea, and I don't know how. I'd have thought he'd have more sense than to be influenced by someone he considers a child, and not a very intelligent one at that!'

'Not intelligent?' Jody coloured and stared at her intently. 'Has Conor said I'm unintelligent?'

A slight pause, and then, a sneer on her lips, 'Certainly he has. And it's the truth—our father soon discovered it, hence the reason he never asked you to come into the business.'

'I was years younger than you,' protested Jody, stung by the idea that Conor considered her lacking in intelligence. 'How could I come into the business?'

'I was in it at sixteen.'

That was indisputable because it was true, and after a moment Rochelle's sneering voice was heard again. 'Well, have you nothing to say?'

'You know I haven't,' replied Jody with a quiet dignity which seemed to set the older girl's teeth on edge. 'If you'll excuse me, I want to sit with Old Bill for a while.'

'If he should by some miracle get better, then I'm going to see that he goes into retirement—'

'You're going to see . . . !' Jody fairly gasped out

the words as fury coloured her cheeks. 'It would seem that I have to remind you yet again that I own half of this hotel and, therefore, I have a large say in what shall happen to Old Bill! You, Rochelle, have no say whatsoever!'

'I soon shall have!'

'You . . . ?' Jody could not ask the question which rose to her lips. Instead, she said quietly, 'If you remember, Rochelle, I did tell you that, when I marry, Turlough will have a say in the running of this hotel. So it would seem that if you do marry Conor, then there will be four of us . . . er . . . dictating to one another.' Rochelle said nothing; her mouth was set, her eyes glinting with wrath. 'As for Old Bill,' Jody continued after a pause, 'as yet, you have no authority over him. Please leave him alone, because I have no intention of allowing you to inflict your arrogance on him anymore.'

'Do you really believe he's going to live?' Amusement and contempt mingled in Rochelle's expression as she added, 'Stop pretending, Jody. Haven't I always said you give yourself away? You know as well as I do that Bill's on his last legs, but you won't admit it.'

'While there's life there's hope!' Jody shot at her, and strode away before Rochelle could taunt her any more with the hopelessness of Old Bill's situation.

The following Thursday Turlough arrived at the castle as usual, but this time he was not taking Jody out to dine; instead he and she were to share in the fun on this 'special night' at the castle, when a medieval banquet had been arranged, mainly for the American guests, who numbered over two hundred —nine-tenths of the entire guest list.

'They love these banquets because they haven't any medieval history of their own,' Esther told Jody when they were chatting one day in the lobby of the hotel. 'We have terrific fun because even though it's all pretence, everyone plays their part by dressing up in old-fashioned clothes.'

Jody had nodded; she knew that the banquets were mentioned in the brochures and, being fore-warned, all guests came prepared to dress for the part they were expected to play. Mr. and Mrs. Pierce from Boston had been chosen as the baron and baroness. They were of Irish descent, as were most of the guests, and they had been delighted when Mr. Pierce's name had been drawn from the box in which all names had been placed.

The baron and baroness sat in state in the centre of the long table set at one end of the vast hall which was kept for occasions such as this. The table was on a raised dais and, in addition to the two most important people, there were their favourites—ladies and gentlemen of quality. Quite naturally, Jody and Conor, Rochelle and Turlough were among those at this top table, with all the other guests seated at tables on a slightly lower level. Serving wenches brought white bibs and, amid up-roarious laughter, fastened them around the necks of the guests. Soup was served in brown wooden bowls and then a main course of meats was served on wooden platters, with only a knife provided, so all were forced to eat with their fingers. Mead was served all the time, also a rich red wine. Guests could have as much as they could drink, and very soon the true atmosphere was created. This was further added to by the four musicians, two men and two women, in period costume, playing harps on a

small stage illuminated by candles, while a jester
added to the fun with his antics.

'This is lovely!' The exclamation was as spontaneous as the smiles Jody was bestowing on the various
serving maids who looked so very different from
the way they looked when serving in the ordinary restaurant. 'How often do we have one of these,
Conor?'

'Not so often now as we used to, I'm afraid.'

'We must have one every two weeks, so that all
the guests will be able to take part.'

'Yes, you're quite right—' began Turlough, when
Rochelle cut across him, saying smoothly, 'If we had
these affairs too often, Conor, there would be no
novelty. Besides, look at the expense. A banquet of
this kind must be far more costly to provide than the
ordinary restaurant menu.'

Jody slanted her a glance from where she sat on
the right of the baroness. So familiar, that kind of
talk! No wonder Philip had been keen to have
Rochelle run his business for him! Nothing was
wasted, neither time nor money. As Rochelle had
previously mentioned, she would dismiss any employee who, in her opinion, was not giving his best to
the firm. And now she would have these banquets
few and far between just for the sake of saving
money.

'I feel as Jody does,' put in Turlough quietly. 'We
should have a banquet once a fortnight so that more
guests would have an opportunity of taking part in
one.'

We. . . . Jody was glad Turlough had used the
word, seeing that Rochelle had done so. Leaning
slightly forward to note Conor's reaction, Jody saw
that his mouth was tight in his angular, rigid profile.

'There appears to be some difference of opinion,' from Rochelle tightly. 'Conor, what is your opinion about this?'

'I haven't given it sufficient thought.' With a lift of his finger Conor brought one of the serving wenches to the table. 'More wine, please, for the baroness.'

'Certainly, sire—at once.' The girl grinned at him, bobbed a curtsy and withdrew.

'This is great fun.' Mr. Pierce was in his element, dressed as the noble baron, master of the castle and all else he surveyed. Entering into the spirit fully, he clapped his hands in a gesture of mock arrogance and a maid came running, then bowed low and said in humble tones, 'Your requirements, sire?'

'More meat, wench!'

Everyone laughed, except Rochelle, who was frowning in thought. And, knowing her so well, Jody was guessing that she was still preoccupied by the cost of the banquets.

And in fact she brought it up again when, after the dessert course of syllabub was served, the guests settled down with a glass of wine to enjoy the show being put on by the dozen or so entertainers who had been engaged for the occasion.

'The cost must be enormous, Conor,' she began, frowning when everyone else was smiling. The baroness turned to stare, and Jody was gratified to see Rochelle colour.

'The cost is well worth it,' stated Turlough in his calm and quiet voice. 'When Jody and I are married, and I come into the business, I shall certainly want these banquets to be put on more often.'

Jody caught her breath, glancing at the baron and his lady, but to her relief, they were far too engrossed in a hilariously funny song about a chastity belt to take any notice of anything else that happened to be going on around them. The man singing the song kept patting his 'wife's' stomach, and there would be a loud rattle of clanging metal followed by a roar of laughter from the audience.

'You hope to make changes here, then?' Conor's voice was like a rasp on steel. 'And do you suppose I would allow those changes?'

'If I come in as husband to your partner, yes, Mr. Blake, you would have to allow the changes.'

Dark threads of crimson were rising under the skin at the sides of Conor's mouth. Jody, horrified by what Turlough had said, tried to catch his eye, but he seemed determined to escape her glance as he added with a half-smile, 'But I daresay we shall all agree in the end. Otherwise the business would suffer, wouldn't it?'

'Aren't you getting a little ahead of things?' demanded Rochelle arrogantly. 'I mean, you and Jody are not even engaged yet—'

'Oh, yes, we are.'

'Then where's Jody's ring?'

'Coming,' answered Turlough briefly, and by his very quietness he gave strength to his words.

Conor was troubled despite his attitude of haughty superiority, for obviously it must have struck him that in future he was not to be the sole organiser of the business. Jody frowned darkly and gave a deep sigh. Turlough had carried things too far, and now it seemed to Jody the only way out was a full confession. What would Conor's opinion be of a trick like that? Jody could not even bear to think about it.

'Turlough,' she whispered unsteadily when at last

she had an opportunity of speaking into his ear, 'you shouldn't have said things like that to Conor.'

'You think not?' There was a very satisfied look on the young man's open face as he added slowly, 'Unless I am very much mistaken, I've done a most profitable piece of work tonight.'

As soon as the banquet was over, Jody bade one quick good night to them all and went to see if Old Bill was comfortable for the night. Although she had offered to look after the old man herself, Conor had insisted on hiring a nurse, who was sleeping in the room next to that occupied by Old Bill. As it was late when Jody went up, the nurse was not with him. Almost silently, Jody opened the bedroom door and trod softly across the carpet to the bed. Bright moonlight flooded through the window, where the curtains were drawn back— on the instructions of Old Bill, who always said he could not abide the shut-in feeling he had when the curtains were closed. Jody stood looking down at the sleeping man, and a great sadness swept through her. He had been her only friend for over twelve years—until she came to Rushwood, where, she believed, she had found another friend in Conor. Now she had Turlough . . . but she was not so sure about Conor anymore. If he married Rochelle, how could he and Jody remain friends?

Old Bill stirred and opened his eyes. 'Little Jody,' he murmured weakly. 'What time is it?'

'After midnight.'

'Was it a good party?'

'Very good. It was something entirely new to me.'

'But you look sad, little Jody.'

'I'll be all right when you are well again,' she returned softly.

'In that case'—the old man smiled—'I'd better be shaping myself up, hadn't I?'

'Yes, you had, Bill.'

'Good night, little Jody,' he said, 'and sleep well.'

'You're all right? You don't need anything—a drink, maybe?'

He shook his head against the pillow. 'Nothing, love—good night again.'

The idea that he was eager to be rid of her had such a disturbing effect on Jody that on sudden impulse she made her way to Conor's suite and knocked on his door. He came at once, tall and handsome as ever, a look of anxious inquiry on his face.

'Old Bill,' she quavered, 'he's . . . worse, I think.'

'I'll come along.' He was closing the door behind him already. 'What makes you think he's worse?'

'The way he wanted me to go.'

Conor lifted an eyebrow. 'Perhaps he wanted the bathroom.'

But Jody shook her head. 'He wasn't intending getting out of bed. I could tell by the way he seemed to snuggle down farther beneath the bedclothes. Conor . . . if . . . if he dies . . .'

'Jody, dear, don't torture yourself with useless conjecture. Old Bill is still very much alive; he's having expert treatment, and even though the doctor's disinclined to say much, there's no reason why we should give up hope, is there?'

'We . . .' Suddenly her eyes glowed, and without

hesitation she laid a hand upon his sleeve. 'Conor, thank you for saying "we." It means that you, too, care about Old Bill.'

'Of course I care,' returned Conor with infinite gentleness. 'He's a most attractive person who has become very well-liked here on the estate.'

'Thank you,' said Jody again, her thoughts flitting to Rochelle and the very different light in which she regarded the old man.

Chapter Ten

The moon had risen on a soft summer night and the atmosphere was surpassingly beautiful as Jody and Conor walked beside the lake. But in contrast to the widespread peace around them, the immediate atmosphere was fraught with tension, with Conor's manner almost frighteningly unfathomable and Jody's nerves stretched as she waited, balanced on a knife edge, for something to happen. Something. . . . But what? Why had he insisted on bringing her out here after he and she had dined in the company of two American guests, Mr. and Mrs. Randall from Texas. The couple had been chatting with Jody and Conor in the lounge over aperitifs, and it seemed natural that Conor should invite them to continue the conversation over dinner and so the two tables were joined. For Jody it was a happy time altogether because Rochelle was once again down with a cold—

hay fever, the doctor had said when, after looking in at Old Bill, he had then at Rochelle's request gone in to see her. That she was furious at the indisposition was more than plain, and that Jody was glad she was laid up was also plain! It was wonderful without Rochelle's dominating the scene all the time, and making herself so conspicuous that glances were repeatedly cast towards the table in the corner.

'I'd like to take a stroll with you, Jody,' Conor had said quietly when, after coffee in the lounge, the Randalls went down to the Dungeon Bar to dance.

'Very well, Conor.' Jody's voice was uneven, because already she was alerted to something un-readable in her partner's manner. The change in him had been dramatic after the departure of the Randalls; he had instantly become serious, almost preoc-cupied. Yet there was a sort of determination about him, as if he were on the brink of some momentous decision or act.

There was a delicate drift of perfume in the air as they came out into a night that was warm and balmy even though autumn was only just around the cor-ner. Conor took Jody's arm as they walked along, leaving the castle lights behind; then she was con-scious of his hand sliding, feather-light, and he was holding her small hand in his, holding it tightly, as if he would never let it go . . . as if he were afraid to let it go. . . .

'Conor,' faltered Jody, impelled to break the silence at last, 'why did you want to come out here with me?'

He slanted her a glance but made no answer, merely tightening his hold after unconsciously slack-ening it a little.

Jody frowned in puzzlement and had to break the

silence again. 'I asked you a question and you didn't answer.'

They were in total isolation on the wooded shores of the lough, and Conor slowed his steps, eventually coming to a halt in a little clearing dappled with shadows. The Corrib shone in the moonlight, its still waters mirroring argent drifts of lacy cloud and a few bright stars. And dominating the scene were the mountains, silhouetted against the sky, dark mountains steeped in history but tonight hauntingly silent and restful.

'Jody . . .' Conor's voice was low and richly Irish. 'I've brought you out here for a reason—but you have guessed that, haven't you?'

She nodded, wishing her throat weren't so dry or her nerves so tightly stretched.

'Yes, but . . .'

'This engagement, Jody—it's nonsense! You can't be in love with Turlough. What made you agree to become engaged to him?'

'I do l-love him—' Her untruth was cut off as Conor gave her a little shake.

'You love me,' he stated firmly, 'and don't you dare deny it!'

'I don't know wh-what this is all about . . .' Jody faltered, confusion bringing tears to her eyes. 'What are you trying to do to me?'

'Make you see sense, child—'

'I'm not a child!' she cried, anger and distress mingling to give a lift to her voice. 'I've told you so many times not to regard me as that!'

He looked at her with a softened expression and said, 'No, you're no longer a child. . . .' And he bent his head, his arms sliding around her quivering frame to bring her close to the warmth and hardness of his body. So gentle was his kiss, so tender the touch of his hand on her throat. 'Put your arms around me, Jody.'

'What are you trying to do to me?' she said again, the catch of tears in her voice. 'Tell me! Say something positive, that I can understand!'

'I love you, Jody,' was the simple reply, and Jody leant away from him, a dazed expression in her eyes. Her legs felt wobbly and the nerves of her stomach were throbbing in sympathy with the overrate beating of her heart.

'I don't believe you,' she began, then stopped. Why should he say he loved her if it were not the truth?

'I can understand your feelings,' admitted Conor gently after a pause. 'When I first saw you, and you seemed so very young and helpless, I instinctively adopted the role of guardian, believing that to be what your great-uncle would have expected of me. Even to kiss you seemed the betrayal of a trust, and I was thoroughly ashamed of myself. Yet all the time I must unconsciously have been falling in love with you, but it was only when you said you were engaged to Turlough that the truth hit me.'

'You knew I'd fallen in love with you,' said Jody without knowing why she should have interrupted at all.

'I believed it to be a crush—'

'Believed it because I was so young!' Heated words, but spoken on a choked little sob of protest.

'I admit it,' returned Conor gently. 'And because I was sorry for you, I tried to make you forget me by favouring Rochelle. It seemed a simple way of curing you, and that was the reason why I said I liked her a lot.'

'It was done to make me see sense? You didn't

really like Rochelle?' Jody's heart was thumping loudly; she felt sure he must hear it, because all was so silent around them.

'I find that as an employee Rochelle is perfect, but as for anything else . . .' He broke off, and she saw him frown in the moonlight. 'That kind of woman has no appeal at all for me.'

'And . . . and it's me you love?' So difficult the words, because her whole being was in a state of quivering doubt and fear. 'Conor, are you serious? Do you really mean it?'

For answer he took her in his arms, bent his head and kissed her gently on the lips. 'I really mean it,' came his answer at last. Jody could not speak for the emotion that affected her senses, and after a small pause Conor said softly, his mouth close to her cheek, 'Will you marry me, darling?'

She lifted her face, her eyes glowing in the moonlight. 'I can't believe it's true.' Her slender body trembled against him, and he held her protectively. 'If it *is* true, then . . . yes, I will marry you . . .' She broke off, shyness robbing her of the words she wanted to utter, so she offered him a tremulous little smile instead.

'My sweet Jody. . . .' Once again Conor bent his head. She felt the yielding of her lips as his mouth slid gently over them; she was aware of the desire in his body and thrilled to the knowledge that it was her own soft pliability that had stirred him. They stood together for a long while in silence, Conor's hands caressing, his lips taking, his voice reassuring in its endearments. At last he held her from him and shook his head.

'I can hardly wait,' he owned with a rueful smile. 'When will you marry me, love?'

'Just whenever you like . . .' Jody stopped abruptly and then said in an absurd little voice. 'What about Turlough—my . . . er . . . fiancé?'

'He's not important.' Conor subjected her to a long hard scrutiny. 'I can't imagine why you became engaged to him when you didn't love him. Perhaps you'll explain?'

'It was . . . was for comfort,' she answered, deliberately avoiding his eyes lest he should guess that she was lying. 'I felt so . . . so alone in the world when . . . when you became interested in Rochelle and almost ignored me.'

'That was the only reason you became engaged to him?'

Was there a sceptical note in his voice? wondered Jody, lifting her eyes at last. 'Yes, that was the only reason.' She hated lying to him, but if she told him the truth, then he would surely despise her.

'And would you have married him?'

'I . . . er . . .'

'Don't you dare lie to me, Jody!'

She made no comment, nor did she answer his question. Instead she went on tiptoe and kissed him full on the lips, hoping to divert his mind from Turlough. She succeeded in a way that left her breathless, for she was swept into his arms, crushed against him and for several ecstatic minutes the pulsing within her increased as his warm hands roamed, and when his body set up waves of rhythmic motion, Jody willingly responded until a violent deluge of ecstasy drove through her and in sudden fear and inexperience she jerked herself away.

His dark eyes smiled down into her flushed face and he said gently, 'You must marry me soon, darling—very soon.' His lips were warm and tender on her throat, his hand gentle on her breast. 'It has to be soon, hasn't it?'

She nodded, but swiftly her thoughts went to Old Bill and she said, grave-faced and sad, 'If anything should happen to Bill, then I couldn't be married for a little while, Conor.' Anxiously, she peered into his eyes. 'You would understand, wouldn't you?'

'Of course, dearest.' His arms became protective as he felt the sudden trembling of her body. 'He's old, Jody, dear, but I feel he will get over this. We must then take good care of him and not let him work very much at all.'

'He'll not accept his wages if he doesn't work.'

'I think we can arrange something.'

'He's so proud.'

'I shall see that his pride isn't hurt.'

'You're a wonderful person,' she whispered huskily. 'Oh, but I do love you!'

'And I love you.' Simple words spoken in tenderness as Conor lowered his mouth to hers. For Jody this was magical, a rapturous interlude which must forever be the most important memory in the whole of her life.

'I must take you in, my love.' Conor's voice broke into her thoughts, and she nodded her head. He took her hand and they walked slowly back into the moonlit gardens of the castle.

It was not until she was in her bedroom that Jody thought of Rochelle and wondered how she would receive the news. That she would be wildly furious was not to be doubted, and Jody felt she must try to keep out of her way until she left the castle. Would she leave right away? It was unlikely that Conor would dismiss her, because he had no idea of the things Rochelle had been saying and Jody now realised that to Rochelle they were all dreams and aspirations rather than realities. For it was certain that Conor had never given Rochelle any encouragement to believe that he was interested in her in any way other than as an employee.

For a long time Jody lay awake, her thoughts flitting from Conor to Old Bill, then to Rochelle, and finally to Turlough, who would be very surprised at what had happened. At last her thoughts began to blur into sleep; she turned on her side and knew nothing more until awakened by the sun pouring through a chink in the drapes.

Her first act after bathing and dressing was to go and see Old Bill, who, to her amazement, was sitting up in bed eating the breakfast of milky porridge given to him by the nurse.

'You might well stare,' he said with a chuckle. 'But didn't I promise to shape myself up?'

'Bill . . .' Slowly, wonderingly, Jody approached the bed. 'How are you feeling?'

'How do I look?'

The nurse came in, a smile on her round, homely face. 'He's going to be all right,' she stated with confidence. 'Good to make the century—and more!'

'It's a miracle!' Another miracle, mused Jody, thinking about last night and the declaration of love made to her by Conor.

'Wait till the doctor comes,' said Old Bill with another satisfied chuckle. 'He was sure I was about to die—'

'Don't!' pleaded Jody swiftly. 'Oh, but this is so marvellous! I must go and tell Conor . . .' Her voice trailed off as a blush swept into her cheeks. 'Bill . . . I'm going to marry Conor. He asked me last night.'

'He did?' Wonderment looked out from the pale lavender eyes. 'Well, little Jody, all your fears have proved to be unfounded, haven't they?'

She nodded and smiled, feeling embarrassed at being reminded of her confessions to Old Bill. 'Yes, it's me he loves and not Rochelle after all.'

'Didn't I tell you it was all nonsense? I knew Mr. Blake would be able to see through that one!'

Jody laughed. The nurse wanted to know if she had heard right, and it was Old Bill who answered. 'Yes, you have heard right. This lovely young lady is going to be married to Mr. Blake.' So proud he sounded; his pale eyes were alive, and on his lips there was a smile of quiet contentment.

Jody could have hugged him if the nurse had not been there. Instead, she said happily, 'I must go and spread the good news of your recovery, Bill. Everyone has been worried about you, especially Mr. Blake and Tommy.'

'Then just you go along and tell them that old soldiers never die!'

'Conor called you that,' she told him huskily. But at the time, she hadn't been as optimistic as he.

The news soon spread that Old Bill had made a miraculous recovery, and when the doctor came he stood by the bed shaking his head in disbelief. 'It must have been willpower,' he was saying to Conor as he left the castle. 'I'd definitely given up hope.'

'He'll not be able to work, though?'

'Not so hard as he would like, no doubt. But it's my belief that he's a man who wouldn't be happy if he were idle.'

'That's just what I said,' interposed Jody on an anxious note. 'You'll let him do something, won't you, dear Conor?'

His smile came swiftly. It was as though he could not deny Jody anything. 'We shall have to find him a light job,' he promised. 'Something in the hotel itself.'

When Rochelle did not put in an appearance at the breakfast table, Jody felt obliged to go and see how she was, and if she wanted anything to eat.

'You can ring down for coffee and toast,' Rochelle said in answer to Jody's inquiry. 'And will you tell Conor I shan't be able to work today but I hope to be all right by morning?'

'Yes, I'll tell him that.'

'He'll probably be up to see me before very long. He was very anxious about me last night.'

'Last night?' Jody had no idea why she asked the question, but she was exceedingly curious to know what kind of an answer she would receive.

'He came to say good night, naturally.' Arrogance in the tone, which was all too familiar to Jody's ears. And the vivid blue eyes held a sort of mocking contempt. Jody looked at her, sitting up against the pillows, and she thought that even in bed like this there was a certain measure of casual elegance and assurance about Rochelle.

'What time did he come up to say good night?' she inquired, feeling specious because she knew that Rochelle was going to lie.

'Oh . . . er . . . around ten or half-past.'

'Conor was with me at that time,' Jody informed her quietly, and watched the colour creep slowly into Rochelle's face.

'It could have been later.' A fractional pause, and then: 'I told you to ring for coffee and toast.'

Jody lifted the telephone receiver and asked for

room service. 'Are you sure you don't want anything else, Rochelle? An egg or some bacon?'

'No, thanks.' Rochelle pressed back against the pillows and regarded her adoptive sister thoughtfully. 'You appear to be very satisfied with yourself this morning,' she said. 'What's happened?'

'Old Bill is as bright as a button.'

'He . . . ' Rochelle stared and frowned, and her lips snapped together. 'Are you sure? I was led to believe there was no hope for him. The doctor—'

'There was always hope! Old Bill will live for many years yet.'

'Well, I hope he won't be *here* for years yet!' said Rochelle tersely. 'Conor must be advised—'

'Conor knows how to run the business, Rochelle. Neither he nor I require help from you.'

'Don't be insolent! What makes you think you can speak for Conor?'

A small pause, and then, quietly and confidently, but yet without one hint of malice: 'Because Conor will soon be my husband, and I know for sure that he is as keen as I am for Old Bill to remain here for the rest of his life.'

'Conor will soon be your husband?' Rochelle stared through widened eyes as the colour began to leave her face. 'What the devil are you trying to put over on me? Conor would never even look at you in that way!' Despite the strength of her words, they totally lacked confidence as she added, 'I don't believe you, Jody—you little liar!'

'I'm not lying,' returned Jody in a quiet, dignified tone. 'Conor loves me and wants to marry me.' Although she had known how Rochelle would feel when told of her engagement to Conor, Jody was not prepared for the expression of sheer venom that settled on Rochelle's face, twisting it into lines so ugly they appeared almost evil, and a shudder passed through Jody's slender frame.

'Loves you . . . ' Suddenly the venom was gone, replaced by a look that immediately sent ripples of apprehension along Jody's spine. She felt breathless as she waited for Rochelle to speak, to say what had just come into her mind. The lovely mouth curved into a sneer and the blue eyes raked Jody's body, contempt within their depths.

'So he proposed, did he? I never thought he'd stoop to anything like that, and yet, looking back, he seemed very perturbed at the idea of your marrying someone else, someone who would come along poking his nose in and telling Conor what to do.' Rochelle stopped and nodded slowly, her brow furrowed as if she were deep in retrospection. 'He spoke to me about his anxiety and said he'd never allow another man to interfere in the running of this hotel. Conor seemed so sure he could prevent it, and this is the way he has chosen.'

A harsh laugh of contempt shot through the ensuing silence before Jody said, a sob in the protesting timbre of her voice, 'It isn't true! You're just causing mischief, because you're jealous! Conor wouldn't hurt me—'

'You're not sure, are you?' jeered Rochelle. 'You'd like to believe he loves you, but yet it's so very plain that his reason for wanting to marry you is to keep Turlough out of the business. With you as his wife, he will gain full control—'

'Stop!' cried Jody, backing towards the door. 'It isn't true! Nothing of what you are saying is true!'

'Isn't it just like you to have been taken in by Conor's smooth talk.' Rochelle threw back her head and laughed. 'Stupid little fool! Father was right when he said you had no intelligence!'

'You told me Conor had said so, but it was a lie! He'd never say a think like that, even if he thought it.'

'Go away, girl. You're so naive you exhaust my patience. Marry him and see what happens to you and your inheritance!'

'I shall marry him, no matter what you think.' Without giving Rochelle an opportunity of saying anything more, Jody opened the door and stepped through it. But once outside, the tears began to fall. Rochelle was right, of course. She, Jody, was just a simpleton who had believed in miracles, accepting without question that Conor had fallen in love with her. But as she dwelt on the entire situation now, she found it easy to form the pattern as described by Rochelle. It was the logical course for Conor to take in the circumstances, believing as he did that she had been intending to marry Turlough. But *had* he believed it? Jody began to wonder as she recalled Conor's question and also his firm assertion that she could not love Turlough because she loved him, Conor.

I'll go and see Turlough, decided Jody, and drying her tears, she went to the telephone. Turlough would meet her that afternoon in Cong, he said, after asking why she wanted to see him. 'I want your opinion about something that has happened,' was all she would say over the telephone, and with that Turlough had to contain his impatience.

She walked to the village and entered the café where Turlough said he would be waiting. He stood up as she entered, and subjected her to a long interrogating stare.

She sat down and he ordered tea and hot buttered scones.

'Conor asked me to marry him,' she told Turlough without preamble. 'It was last night—'

'By Jove!' he cut in excitedly. 'I'd worked for some reaction but never had I envisaged his coming that kind of stunt! He wants control, wants to make sure no other man shall come along and interfere. Well, I don't know what you intend to do, but between us we've done the trick. We've drawn him away from Rochelle once and for all!'

'You . . . you believe he wants to . . . to marry me j-just to gain full control of the hotel?' Jody wondered if she were as pale as she felt, or if her trembling was visible. Her heart was like lead, her spirits just about as low as they could be.

'It's obvious, isn't it?'

Mutely, Jody nodded her head. What a fool she had been! Rochelle was right when she described her as naive.

And Conor . . . such behaviour seemed completely out of character . . . and yet, it was the natural course to take, the only one from his point of view.

'Are you going to marry him?' Turlough wanted to know, and when she did not answer immediately, he added curiously, 'What did Conor say about me? After all, you and I *are* supposed to be engaged.'

'He seemed very sure I'd give you up,' was all Jody returned in answer to that.

'Well, are you going to marry him?' asked Turlough again.

'I don't know.' A shuddering sigh escaped her. 'I just don't know what to do.'

'You love him, Jody, so your choice should be

easy.' Turlough's voice was as gentle as the hand with which he covered hers. 'He's a good man, dear, and I am sure he'll treat you kindly.'

'I would want more than kindness,' she quavered.

'Did he say he loved you?'

'Yes—' she nodded—'he did.'

'Perhaps he was speaking the truth.' Turlough's brow furrowed in thought. 'We haven't considered that aspect, have we? I merely jumped to the obvious conclusion, which was that he wished for full control of the business he had been running for years anyway. But if he says he loves you . . .'

'He'd have to, wouldn't he?' Jody caught her underlip between her teeth in an effort to hold back the tears. 'Rochelle was right. He just wants to use me for his own ends.'

'Rochelle?'—sharply and with a swift interrogating glance.

Jody related all that Rochelle had said, watching his frown appear, then deepen, watching the compression of his mouth.

'It was because of what she'd said earlier that you came to me?'

'Yes. I had to come to find out your reaction—'

'And it served to strengthen suspicions already rooted in your mind by Rochelle.' Anger in his voice now, anger against himself. But it soon passed, and when he spoke, his voice was as soft and gentle as ever. 'Marry him, Jody, dear . . . and be happy.'

'I don't know—I can't make up my mind!'

'I want you to promise me you'll marry him.' Turlough's hand pressed firmly over the back of hers as he spoke. 'Promise, right now.'

She considered a moment, seeing Rochelle's triumph if she should turn Conor down, influenced by the malicious barbs of doubt which Rochelle had shot into her mind.

'I promise,' said Jody in a firm, decisive voice. 'Yes, I shall marry him.'

'Rochelle, aren't you leaving here, now that Conor and I are to be married?' It was three days later that Jody asked the question after having waited with confident expectation for Rochelle to hand in her notice to Conor. She had come upon Rochelle in the grounds of the castle; she had been standing by a little walled retreat, looking out over the lough to where the white pleasure boat was just passing one of the islands.

'No, I'm not leaving,' was the immediate reply, thrown out in arrogance not unmingled with a hint of triumph, which was both puzzling and disturbing to Jody. 'Even if Conor were to marry you, it wouldn't last six months, and I'd be around when the break came. However,' she continued after a slight pause, 'when I've spoken to Conor and told him what I know, there won't be any marriage.'

'What do you know?' There was a hint of bravado in Jody's voice, with nothing to betray the fact that fear was sending ripples along her spine.

'You and Turlough entered into a conspiracy to bring about a split between Conor and me!' Suddenly all control left Rochelle, black fury entering eyes already dark with jealousy and hate. 'Admit it!' she rasped. 'Admit that you and Turlough never had any intention of marrying. You and he merely conspired to force Conor's hand! Turlough was the clever one, though. I soon guessed it was his idea originally—yes, you might well blush, girl! You always did give yourself away, didn't you?' Rochelle stopped, emotion causing her mouth to twist into a shape so ugly it was hardly recognisable. 'A conspiracy to frighten Conor into some sort of action! He'd have been mine!' snarled Rochelle viciously. 'And he still will be, because I intend to give your little game away!'

'You're . . . you're assuming a . . . a great deal,' quavered Jody, white to the lips. 'Conor said he loved me, and it could be true—'

'He could scarcely give you the real reason for wanting to marry you, could he?'

'I have no proof that he wants to marry me solely to gain full control of the business. The more I think of it, the less I can reconcile that kind of behaviour with a man as honourable and upright as Conor.'

'He's first and foremost a businessman. From his point of view, his only course is to marry you—or so he believes at the present time. But when I've told him what a conniving little wretch you are, he'll realise there's no need for him to go to the lengths of marrying you, simply because you never had any intention of marrying Turlough.'

'You appear to know so much . . . ' Jody's voice trailed off and her eyes dilated as Conor emerged from behind the wall, his face tight with anger. Rochelle faced him triumphantly, while Jody shrank back against the wall, conscious of the fine hairs on her arms lifting as a terrible feeling of fear and defeat took possession of both mind and body.

His anger was against her; it must be, she thought miserably as she listened to Rochelle say, 'You heard, Conor?' There was a tinge of apprehension in her voice, and it struck Jody that for all her cool triumphant exterior, Rochelle was a little frightened, too, in case Conor had heard *all* of what she had been saying. 'You were in the retreat?'

Tall and forbidding, he looked down into Rochelle's lovely eyes and seemed to be examining them with a strange intensity, as if looking for something he had previously missed. And then, strangely, he gave a little shrug of his wide shoulders and said at length, 'Yes, I heard.' He turned his attention to Jody, who dropped her eyes beneath his stare. 'Jody, I think you and I need to talk in private—'

'But if you heard, Conor,' began Rochelle, a winning smile on her lips, 'then you must know you've been cheated. I managed to sort the whole thing out, and the result was—'

'Rochelle,' broke in Conor with dangerous quiet, 'I'm dismissing you without the customary notice. If you see Esther in about half an hour's time, she'll have your full month's salary. I shall expect you to leave the castle before dinner.' Conor turned his back on her, so it was only Jody who saw the look of sheer hatred and jealousy that twisted the elder girl's lovely face. 'Jody, come with me!' said Conor peremptorily. 'Into my study.'

A few minutes later he was asking if what he had heard was true.

'About the conspiracy?' Jody nodded without lifting her head. 'Yes, Conor, it was all true.'

'You and Turlough never did intend to marry?' Although a question, it seemed to be a statement as well. 'I see . . .'

Something in his tone of voice caused Jody's heart to beat a little faster. She looked up into his face and saw that all anger had left it. Bewildered, she asked, 'Aren't you very angry with me, Conor?'

'Tell me,' he said, bypassing the question, 'what was the reason for the conspiracy?'

'Must I tell you?'

'You must, Jody.'

She paused, but only momentarily, for she knew Conor well enough to be sure he would make her do as he wished. 'It was Rochelle,' she began, then went on to tell him everything her adoptive sister had said and done. She left nothing out—and in any case, he had heard much from Rochelle's lips anyway, out there by the retreat.

'And so when Turlough heard all this from you, he had the bright idea of pretending he was to come in, as your husband, and interfere in the running of the hotel.' Conor spoke after a long silent moment, and then a low laugh escaped him which brought the question again to Jody's lips, 'Aren't you angry?'

'Come here, my love . . . ' But it was he who moved, drawing closer to take her gently into his arms. 'You were right, my darling, when you told Rochelle that it could be true that I loved you. But it's plain that you did doubt my motives.'

'Yes, I did,' she had to admit. 'You see, after Rochelle had said all those things, it did seem that she was right in what she had surmised. I just had to go to see Turlough, who was of the same opinion as Rochelle at first. He believed you were marrying me to gain full control of the business.'

'At first,' repeated Conor, ignoring the rest.

'Yes, but afterwards he said you could very well be speaking the truth when you said you loved me. Turlough made me promise to marry you. I don't think he'd have let me go if I hadn't.'

'A most perceptive young man. I owe him a special thank-you.' Connor paused to kiss her and then asked curiously, 'How was it that Turlough didn't fall in love with you?'

'He guessed, almost from the first, that I loved you.'

'And I suppose you let him hold you for comfort?'

Jody nodded reflectively. 'I needed someone, Conor,' she returned huskily. 'I felt so shut out and lost . . . '

'But never again, my darling!' His mouth was cool and strong on her lips, his arms tender and protective about her quivering body. 'I can now understand why you were so upset when I took Rochelle on as my secretary. Dearest, why didn't you confide in me?'

'You were fighting your love for me at that time,' Jody reminded him. 'If I'd known you loved me, then of course I would have confided . . . ' She paused as a lovely smile transformed her face. ' . . . just as I will always confide in the future, dearest Conor, because you are the only one who loves and understands me.' But then she remembered Old Bill and felt she was doubly blessed.

'There will be others,' he assured her tenderly, and because she knew what he meant, a soft blush rose to her cheeks. Children . . . Conor's and hers, brought up in this beautiful setting . . . children who would be loved and would love in return.

'Old Bill will be so happy if I—we—have children,' she murmured. 'He's missed so much in life.'

'Well, from now on he isn't going to miss anything. Thank God he's recovered, and from what the doctor said when I rang him earlier today, it would seem the nurse was right—he's good for the century.' After that it seemed that Conor had no intention of talking about Old Bill, or anyone else for that matter, for his lips became fixed to Jody's in a kiss that was both savage and tender, possessive, and yet there was a certain reverence in it which came over Jody and thrilled her as much as the dominance of his hands as they caressed her curves, then crushed her to him, melding her soft young body with the granite hardness of his sinewed frame, bringing her so close that she was vitally aware of his sudden need for her and she arched convulsively, revelling in the intimacy, the primordial yearning which she knew was affecting them both with equal intensity. His hands moved again, roving hands bent on exploring and conquering, and for Jody it was a dangerous moment when presently his fingers curled round one small firm breast, masterfully arousing a desire which brought forth a little moan of ecstasy from lips that were still surrendering to the dominance of his.

'My beloved . . . ' Conor's voice was hoarse and thick against her throat, his warm hands sliding possessively along her thighs. 'Dearest Jody, I adore you!'

Jody's own response was eloquent in its simplicity, for she could only murmur, 'Thank you for loving me,' before, with a tiny sigh of contentment, she found a place for her head on his chest.

THE NEW NAME IN LOVE STORIES

Six new titles every month bring you the best in romance. Set all over the world, exciting and brand new stories about people falling in love:

Silhouette Romance

THE NEW NAME IN LOVE STORIES

Silhouette Romance

THE NEW NAME IN LOVE STORIES

Silhouette *Romance*

EXCITING MEN,
EXCITING PLACES, HAPPY ENDINGS . . .

Contemporary romances for today's women

If there's room in your life for a little more romance,
SILHOUETTE ROMANCES are for you.

And you won't want to miss a single one so start
your collection now.

Each month, six very special love stories will be yours
from SILHOUETTE

32687 5	RENEGADE PLAYER Dixie Browning No.142	75p
32688 3	SONG OF THE WEST Nora Roberts No.143	75p
32689 1	A NEW DAWN Ellen Goforth No.144	75p
32690 5	LOVE CAPTIVE Jacqueline Hope No.145	75p
32691 3	NIGHTSTAR Fern Michaels No.146	75p

*All these books are available at your local bookshop or newsagent, or
can be ordered direct from the publisher. Just tick the titles you want and
fill in the form below.*

Prices and availability subject to change without notice.

SILHOUETTE BOOKS, P.O. Box 11, Falmouth, Cornwall.

Please send cheque or postal order, and allow the following for postage
and packing:

U.K. – 45p for one book, plus 20p for the second book, and 14p for
each additional book ordered up to a £1.63 maximum.

B.F.P.O. and EIRE – 45p for the first book, plus 20p for the second
book, and 14p per copy for the next 7 books, 8p per book thereafter.

OTHER OVERSEAS CUSTOMERS – 75p for the first book, plus
21p per copy for each additional book.

Name ....

Address ....

....

His smile came swiftly. It was as though he could not deny Jody anything. 'We shall have to find him a light job,' he promised. 'Something in the hotel itself.'

When Rochelle did not put in an appearance at the breakfast table, Jody felt obliged to go and see how she was, and if she wanted anything to eat.

'You can ring down for coffee and toast,' Rochelle said in answer to Jody's inquiry. 'And will you tell Conor I shan't be able to work today but I hope to be all right by morning?'

'Yes, I'll tell him that.'

'He'll probably be up to see me before very long. He was very anxious about me last night.'

'Last night?' Jody had no idea why she asked the question, but she was exceedingly curious to know what kind of an answer she would receive.

'He came to say good night, naturally.' Arrogance in the tone, which was all too familiar to Jody's ears. And the vivid blue eyes held a sort of mocking contempt. Jody looked at her, sitting up against the pillows, and she thought that even in bed like this there was a certain measure of casual elegance and assurance about Rochelle.

'What time did he come up to say good night?' she inquired, feeling specious because she knew that Rochelle was going to lie.

'Oh . . . er . . . around ten or half-past.'

'Conor was with me at that time,' Jody informed her quietly, and watched the colour creep slowly into Rochelle's face.

'It could have been later.' A fractional pause, and then: 'I told you to ring for coffee and toast.'

Jody lifted the telephone receiver and asked for

room service. 'Are you sure you don't want anything else, Rochelle? An egg or some bacon?'

'No, thanks.' Rochelle pressed back against the pillows and regarded her adoptive sister thoughtfully. 'You appear to be very satisfied with yourself this morning,' she said. 'What's happened?'

'Old Bill is as bright as a button.'

'He . . . ' Rochelle stared and frowned, and her lips snapped together. 'Are you sure? I was led to believe there was no hope for him. The doctor—'

'There was always hope! Old Bill will live for many years yet.'

'Well, I hope he won't be *here* for years yet!' said Rochelle tersely. 'Conor must be advised—'

'Conor knows how to run the business, Rochelle. Neither he nor I require help from you.'

'Don't be insolent! What makes you think you can speak for Conor?'

A small pause, and then, quietly and confidently, but yet without one hint of malice: 'Because Conor will soon be my husband, and I know for sure that he is as keen as I am for Old Bill to remain here for the rest of his life.'

'Conor will soon be your husband?' Rochelle stared through widened eyes as the colour began to leave her face. 'What the devil are you trying to put over on me? Conor would never even look at you in that way!' Despite the strength of her words, they totally lacked confidence as she added, 'I don't believe you, Jody—you little liar!'

'I'm not lying,' returned Jody in a quiet, dignified tone. 'Conor loves me and wants to marry me.' Although she had known how Rochelle would feel when told of her engagement to Conor, Jody was not prepared for the expression of sheer venom that